**As he walked o[...]**
**double doors he [...]**
**recognised, saying [...]**
**Miss Beautiful. Let's go and meet**
**Daddy.'**

*Daddy?*

Max couldn't help looking, and immediately wished he hadn't. Because at the far end of the corridor Marina was carrying a toddler: a little girl who had the same dark hair, dark eyes and sweet smile as Marina herself.

*Marina had a daughter.*

For a moment Max couldn't breathe; it felt as if someone had just sucker-punched him in the stomach and all the air had been driven out of his lungs. Especially when a man came walking down the corridor towards them, kissed Marina lightly, and scooped the child from her arms.

'Daddy!' the little girl said, beaming as he kissed her and lifted her onto his shoulders.

Marina tucked her arm through his and they walked off together, chatting easily. Looking exactly like the close, loving family they obviously were.

Exactly like the close, loving family he and Marina had planned to be.

**Kate Hardy** lives in Norwich, in the east of England, with her husband, two young children, one bouncy spaniel, and too many books to count! When she's not busy writing romance or researching local history, she helps out at her children's schools. She also loves cooking—spot the recipes sneaked into her books! (They're also on her website, along with extracts and stories behind the books.) Writing for Mills & Boon has been a dream come true for Kate—something she wanted to do ever since she was twelve. She's been writing Medical™ Romances for nearly five years now, and also writes for Modern Heat™. She says it's the best of both worlds, because she gets to learn lots of new things when she's researching the background to a book: add a touch of passion, drama and danger, a new gorgeous hero every time, and it's the perfect job!

Kate's always delighted to hear from readers, so do drop in to her website at www.katehardy.com

**Recent titles by the same author:**

**Medical™ Romance**
FALLING FOR THE PLAYBOY MILLIONAIRE
  *The Brides of Penhally Bay*
THE CHILDREN'S DOCTOR'S SPECIAL
  PROPOSAL
  *The London Victoria*
THE GREEK DOCTOR'S NEW-YEAR BABY
  *The London Victoria*

**Modern Heat™**
TEMPORARY BOSS, PERMANENT MISTRESS
PLAYBOY BOSS, PREGNANCY OF PASSION
  *To Tame a Playboy*
SURRENDER TO THE PLAYBOY SHEIKH
  *To Tame a Playboy*

# THE DOCTOR'S
# LOST-AND-FOUND
# BRIDE

BY
KATE HARDY

MILLS & BOON®

First published in Great Britain 2010
Large Print edition 2010
Harlequin Mills & Boon Limited,
Eton House, 18-24 Paradise Road,
Richmond, Surrey TW9 1SR

ISBN: 978 0 263 21107 8

Harlequin Mills & Boon policy is to use papers that are
natural, renewable and recyclable products and made
from wood grown in sustainable forests. The logging and
manufacturing process conform to the legal environmental
regulations of the country of origin.

Printed and bound in Great Britain
by CPI Antony Rowe, Chippenham, Wiltshire

# THE DOCTOR'S LOST-AND-FOUND BRIDE

# CHAPTER ONE

'EXCUSE me. I couldn't help overhearing the shouting. I'm coming in.'

Marina froze as she heard the voice on the other side of the curtain.

No; of course it wasn't him.

Apart from anything else, Max Fenton didn't work at the London Victoria. So it was completely ridiculous that she'd think he was standing on the other side of the curtain. And she was furious with herself for, yet again, hearing a slightly posh voice and thinking immediately of her ex.

After four years, she should be over him—completely over him. Yet every time she had an oblique view of a man with dark hair that flopped over his forehead, every time she heard someone who sounded faintly like him, she immediately thought of Max. And every time it turned out to be a stranger and she ended up cross with herself for being such a fool.

Of course he wouldn't have followed her to London—not after all this time. He'd signed the divorce papers a year ago, and they'd been separated for three years before that. Sure, Eve had said something about a new senior registrar taking over from Ed, but she hadn't mentioned his name and, as far as Marina knew, the new doctor wasn't starting until next week.

And then the curtain to the cubicle twitched open.

Shock kept her silent.

Since when had Max been working at the London Victoria?

He was definitely staff. Apart from the fact that he was wearing a white coat with a stethoscope flung casually around his neck, his name-badge sported the hospital logo and his name was printed underneath his photograph. But how on earth had she missed the news that he'd joined the team?

She stared at him. There were lines she didn't

remember etched on his face, and he was thinner. Too thin. But his hair was just the same, still flopping over his forehead. And she'd forgotten just how blue his eyes were, a smoky, slate-blue that still managed to make her heart miss a beat when she looked at him, even after all the mess and misery that had happened between them.

For one crazy moment, Marina almost reached out to touch him, to press her palm against his cheek and make absolutely sure that he was really here, that this wasn't some weird kind of hallucination.

But she didn't have the right to touch him. Not any more. For all she knew, he could be married. *With a child.*

The pain at that thought was so intense that she nearly gasped out loud. Then anger bubbled up to block out the pain. What the hell was he doing here? There were plenty of other hospitals in the world. Why did Max have to muscle into hers, push his way back into her life?

Max's face was completely unreadable. She had no idea what he was thinking, or whether he was filled with the same confusing mixture of pain, anger and longing that she was.

He glanced at Marina's name-badge before turning to the woman who'd been yelling at her; when he spoke, his voice was clipped, and made it very clear that he was in charge. 'You're disturbing the other patients. I suggest you leave, so Dr Petrelli can concentrate on treating her patient—or do I need to call security to escort you out?'

The woman curled her lip at him and continued to chew gum loudly. 'It's all *wrong*, that lot coming over here and taking jobs off English people.'

'Not that it's any of your business,' Max said, 'but Dr Petrelli is as English as you are. And, even if she wasn't, this department operates a zero-tolerance policy. Our staff have the right to do their job without abuse.'

'I know my rights,' Ms Gum-Chewer said, folding her arms. 'And you're not getting away with bullying me.'

'The way you're bullying my staff, you mean? Three seconds and I'll be calling security to escort you out. Or you can step outside and let

Dr Petrelli treat your friend without interruptions. Your choice.' He gave her an implacable stare. 'One…two…'

'I'll be just out here, Ally. And you make sure she treats you properly.' The gum-chewing woman sniffed loudly and stalked out of the cubicle.

Grumbling, and with a last, hostile look at Marina, the woman left the cubicle.

Marina still hadn't got over the fact that Max had called her *his* staff.

Ha; she'd stopped being *his* anything a long time ago.

'May I have a word?' Max looked at Marina and gestured to the cubicle curtain.

'Excuse me, Mrs Marshall,' Marina said to her patient. 'I'll be back in just a moment.'

Max closed the curtain behind them. 'Are you all right?'

His voice was formal and polite. How different it had been when they'd first met. She'd been a fresh-faced graduate in her first job as a pre-registered house officer. Everyone had been rushed off their feet on the first day, and Max had introduced himself swiftly in the five-minute break she'd managed to take, before giving her half a chocolate bar to keep her going, along with a cup of lukewarm coffee that she could gulp straight down. His warm, open smile had turned her weak at the knees, and she'd discovered that love at first sight wasn't a myth at all. She'd fallen dizzily, headlong in love with Max Fenton within seconds of meeting him.

But a lot had happened in those five years. And, given their shared past, and the fact that they were clearly going to have to work together, polite, formal and distant was definitely the best way forward.

She glanced at his name-badge again to check his rank and what she should call him. 'Senior registrar': so he *was* the guy who'd taken over from Ed. Still 'doctor' rather than 'mister', then. Odd, because he'd been so focused on his career that she'd expected him to make consultant at a scarily young age. 'I'm fine, thank you, Dr Fenton.'

That was a complete lie. Seeing him again had made her feel as if she'd just ridden an enormous rollercoaster—at double speed, and sitting backwards. She managed to pull herself together. Just. 'Thank you for coming to my rescue.'

'Not a problem.' He gave her an equally cool nod. 'I'll let you get back to your patient.'

'I'm really sorry,' the woman on the bed said when Marina returned to the cubicle. She bit her lip. 'Claire's really kind-hearted.'

Maybe, on her own terms; Marina forbore to comment.

'It's just that sometimes she can come on a bit strong.'

That was putting it mildly, but it wasn't Mrs Marshall's fault that her friend was so overbearing. 'I've had worse—you should see the bad-tempered drunks who end up in here on a Friday night,' Marina said with a smile, wanting to put her patient at her ease. 'Don't worry about it.'

'It's because her husband always looks at your bit in the paper on a Wednesday—he fancies you something rotten,' Mrs Marshall confided.

'I'm very flattered,' Marina said, 'But your friend really doesn't have anything to worry about.' Even if she had been in the market for a relationship—and right now life was too complicated for her to cope with dating someone—she only ever went out with single men.

'I've told her how much Stewie loves her, but she's convinced he's going to look elsewhere because of her weight.' Mrs Marshall sighed and shook her head. 'She's trying so hard to make herself look good for him. She put on three stone when she stopped smoking. That's why she chews gum all the time—to stop herself going back on the ciggies.'

Marina knew that people with low self-esteem often lashed out at others as a way of making themselves feel better. Though it still hurt when you were the one they decided to pick on. 'She's done the right thing for her health, giving up the cigarettes. But we really should talk about *you* rather than your friend,' she said gently. 'I think you've broken your wrist, Mrs Marshall. From what you've told me about the way you landed, and the way your wrist looks, I think you have what's called a Colles' fracture. I'm going to give you some pain relief to make you more comfortable, then send you for an X-ray. When I've had a look at your X-ray and I'm happy that everything's straightforward, I'll put a temporary plaster on your wrist to keep it stable until the fracture clinic can see you.'

'You mean I'm going to be in plaster?' Mrs Marshall looked shocked.

'Modern casts are really lightweight,' Marina reassured her. 'But, yes, you'll need a cast for a few weeks, while your wrist heals.'

'Will I be able to go back to work?'

'It depends what you do for a living. If you use that hand a lot, then it's a good idea to have some time off to let your wrist heal properly. And I'd definitely say no lifting or carrying.'

Mrs Marshall looked upset. 'I don't get paid if I don't work.'

'But if you go back too early, and put too much weight on the fracture, there's a strong chance you'll make it worse and you'll be off work for even longer,' Marina said gently. 'I know it's not going to make you feel much better, but you're the fourth patient I've seen today with a Colles' fracture. When it's icy like this, no end of people slip, put their hands out to save themselves and end up breaking their wrists.'

She gave Mrs Marshall some painkillers, then directed her to X-ray. 'Come back when you've had the X-ray and I'll finish treating you,' she said with a smile.

Max grabbed a file and started to read his next patient's notes, needing a couple of minutes to get himself back under control. When he'd heard someone shouting in the cubicles, and realised that someone was haranguing one of his colleagues, he'd instinctively gone to the rescue.

What he hadn't expected was to see his ex-wife standing there.

He'd had no idea that Marina even worked at the London Victoria, so he hadn't been prepared to face her again. It was a double shock to see her again for the first time in four years.

She was still as gorgeous as ever, with that long, silky, dark hair he'd so loved playing with, albeit tied back for work; those expressive, dark eyes, and the perfect rosebud mouth he'd fallen in love with the very first day he'd met her. She was twenty-eight now, but still looked younger than her years, all soft skin and lush curves. Just as she'd done the first time he'd met her, she'd taken his breath away.

He only hoped that it hadn't shown on his face.

Then again, Max had spent months stuck in a hospital bed with nothing to do except brood and teach himself to mask his feelings. Between that, and three years of working for Doctors Without Borders, he was pretty sure he could keep his expression blank and professional in just about any situation.

Including unexpectedly coming face-to-face again with the love of his life.

He'd told himself that he was ready to work in England again, that he was over Marina. But seeing her just now had taught him how wrong he'd been. He wasn't over her at all. He never had been, and if he were honest with himself he probably never would be.

Not that he was going to do anything about it. Marina's expression had been pretty clear—shock, followed by hurt and anger. Given that she'd been the one to start divorce proceedings, it was obvious that she'd keep her distance from him. For all he knew, she could be in a serious relationship—married, even. He hadn't noticed a ring on her left hand; then again, he'd been too busy trying to look professional and detached to think of even looking. The idea of seeing another man's ring there made him feel sick to the stomach, but what right did he have to protest? He'd signed the papers, after all, agreed to end their marriage instead of fighting for it.

He'd been angry when he'd signed them—angry with Marina for walking out on him, and angry with himself for not doing more to keep them together. But he knew now that the anger had been just a mask for the hurt, something to cover the pit of loss so he couldn't see how deep it was.

He swallowed hard. What a mess. Now they were going to have to work together, and there was a fair chance that they'd be rostered onto the same team in Resus. So, for both their sakes, he was going to have to keep a lid on his feelings and pretend they'd never met before.

Thank God he'd chosen to specialise in emergency medicine, where he'd be kept way too busy to think about his ex-wife. He strode out to the reception area and called his next patient.

\* \* \*

As always, when the weather was icy, the waiting area in the department was standing-room only. Most of the patients had fallen; some were badly bruised, but there were several with Colles' fractures that needed backslabs to keep the break stable before referral to the fracture clinic. But even though Marina was too busy to have a proper break she made sure she spent enough time with each patient to reassure them—particularly one elderly patient who suffered from osteoporosis and had cracked both arms and a hip. Rather than sending her up to the geriatric ward with a porter, Marina took the old lady herself and spent time settling her in to the ward.

Lunch was a sandwich eaten while sorting paperwork between patients. Halfway through the afternoon, Eve, the charge nurse, caught Marina before she saw her next case. 'You haven't had a break today. Go and grab a coffee.'

'We're busy,' Marina protested. 'And you haven't had a break either, Eve.' Nobody in the department did when it was as busy as this. There just wasn't time.

'Go and grab a coffee,' Eve directed. 'You need a break. And you're off at five today, yes?'

Marina nodded. 'I feel awful, leaving early when we've still got a full waiting-room.'

'You were in at eight, and you haven't stopped since you've been in. So leaving at five isn't exactly leaving *early*, is it? And we all know where you're going to be, anyway, if we need you.'

Yes. Picking up Phoebe, then going upstairs to the maternity department and spending a while at her elder sister's bedside.

Eve smiled at her. 'How's Rosie doing?'

'Getting there. She's feeling well enough to moan about being stuck in here and wanting to be at home with Neil and Phoebe.'

'That's a good sign. And the baby's doing OK?'

'Doing fine.' Marina bit her lip. 'Though I think we'll all be a lot happier when he or she's here safely.'

'Rosie's in good hands. You know as well as I do, Theo Petrakis is the best.' Eve patted her shoulder. 'Now, scoot.'

'Five minutes and I'll be back.'

'Make it fifteen,' Eve said.

Marina had no intention of taking that long, not when they were so busy. But she went through to the staff kitchen, made herself a mug of coffee and added enough cold water so that she could drink it quickly.

'Is the kettle still hot?' a voice behind her asked, and she nearly dropped her mug.

*Max.*

Longing surged through her, but she stifled it. Fast. 'Yes, Dr Fenton.' She forced herself to sound cool, calm and professional; the last thing she wanted was for him to realise that his voice was enough to turn her to a gibbering mess inside.

If there was an atmosphere between them people would start asking questions. Marina really didn't want to be the hot topic on the hospital grapevine. So, much as she hated it, she forced herself to make small talk. 'I didn't know you were going to be working here,' she said.

'I had an interview two weeks ago,' Max replied, making himself a coffee and topping it up with cold water, the same way Marina had.

Two weeks ago: that explained it. Life had been

so crazy since Rosie had been admitted to the maternity ward with pre-eclampsia sixteen days before that Marina really hadn't paid much attention to what was going on at work. She just did her shift, visited her sister before and after every shift and helped her brother-in-law Neil to look after Phoebe, Rosie and his two-year-old daughter.

'I didn't realise you were here, either,' Max added. 'You weren't here when I had a tour of the department.'

'I was probably off duty.' Not that he needed to know what she'd been doing. He hadn't kept in touch with her family at all; as far as she was concerned, he wasn't part of her family any longer, and she didn't owe him any explanations.

'How long have you been working here?'

'Nearly a year.' She glanced at him, and was gratified to see a slight flicker in his eyes. Good: so he *did* remember what had happened a year ago. He'd taken long enough to sign the divorce papers. Her solicitor had had to send them to him three times because he hadn't bothered replying; the ending of their marriage had clearly been as low a priority in his life as their marriage itself.

But at last she was free. She'd gone back to using her maiden name. At the London Victoria, they'd only ever known her as Marina Petrelli—and that was the way she wanted it to stay.

'It's a good place to work,' she said.

He raised an eyebrow. 'Is it going to be a problem, my working here?'

Trust Max to cut to the chase.

Yes, it was a problem. She'd much rather they didn't have to work together. But she couldn't change the situation, only make the best of it. 'I think,' she said carefully, 'We're both profes-sional enough to put our patients first.'

'Good.'

There was a long, long pause. Marina couldn't think of a single thing to say.

Actually, that wasn't true. There was a lot she wanted to say. Answers she wanted to demand. But the emergency-department kitchen wasn't the right place to say any of it.

If anyone had said to her five years ago that she'd find it difficult to talk to Max, she would've laughed in disbelief. They'd never stopped talking, right from the start. And Max had fitted right in to her noisy, talkative family. The Petrellis had adored him as much as she had.

Until their marriage had gone so badly wrong. Then she and Max had stopped talking completely.

*Marry in haste, repent at leisure:* how horribly true that saying had turned out to be.

'Well, I'd better get back,' she said, rinsing out her mug and trying to avoid eye contact.

'Me, too.'

*Oh, no. Please don't let him suggest walking back to the department together.* She wasn't ready for this. But, to her relief, Max was still finishing his coffee, which meant she could escape.

'Bye, then,' she said brightly, and left the room.

How on earth had they come to this point? Max wondered. They were awkward, embarrassed strangers who could barely make small talk in a staff kitchen.

Though he knew exactly how they'd got here:

through pain and hurt that they'd both been too young to deal with at the time. Marina had walked out and gone home to her parents for the comfort he hadn't been able to give her. And he'd responded by going off to work for Doctors Without Borders, where he'd known he'd be too busy to think about the wreck of their marriage.

And now they had to work together. He'd seen on her face that, yes, it was a problem for her. It was a problem for him, too. But they'd better deal with it—and fast—because he sure as hell didn't want to be the subject of the hospital grapevine. He'd been there before and he wasn't in any hurry to repeat the experience: people whispering and stopping conversations dead as soon as they saw him walk in, the pitying glances.

If he'd known that she worked here, he wouldn't have taken the job.

Then again, this had been too good an opportunity to turn down: a position as senior registrar in a busy London emergency-department. Added to his experience abroad, it would stand him in good stead for future promotion, for the consultant's post that was the focus of his life right now.

Luckily the rest of his afternoon was too rushed to let Max think about Marina. There were several victims of road-traffic accidents who needed checking over—including one with broken ribs and a pneumothorax that needed very careful attention. Even so, he was aware that Marina left the department a good half-hour before he did.

Then, as he walked out through the double doors, he heard a voice he recognised, saying cheerfully, 'Right, Miss Beautiful. Let's go and meet Daddy.'

*Daddy?*

Max couldn't help looking, and immediately wished he hadn't. Because at the far end of the corridor Marina was carrying a toddler: a little girl who had the same dark hair, dark eyes and sweet smile as Marina herself.

*Marina had a daughter.*

For a moment, Max couldn't breathe; it felt as if someone had just sucker-punched him in the stomach and all the air had been driven out of his lungs. The little girl looked as if she was around two years old—which meant that Marina hadn't even waited for their divorce to be finalised before she'd moved on to another relationship and had a baby with her new partner.

Yet she still used her maiden name in the department. Maybe she hadn't yet remarried. Or maybe she'd decided to keep her maiden name for work.

Whatever.

It was none of his business any more.

All the same, it shook him. Especially when a man came walking down the corridor towards them, kissed Marina lightly on the mouth and scooped the child from her arms.

'Daddy!' the little girl said, beaming as the man kissed her and lifted her onto his shoulders.

Marina tucked her arm through his and they walked off together, chatting easily. Looking exactly like the close, loving family they obviously were.

Exactly like the close, loving family he and Marina had planned to have.

Max swallowed the bile that had risen in his

throat. Now he understood why Marina had left her shift dead on time. She'd had to pick up her daughter from the hospital nursery before meeting her partner.

What made the whole thing so much worse was that, if circumstances had been very slightly different, Max would've been the one meeting Marina with a bright, lively pre-school child, and maybe a baby with chubby hands and a wide, wide smile. He would've been the one they smiled at, the one they greeted with a kiss.

He swore under his breath. He'd promised himself that he was over it, that he could cope with working in England again. But seeing that little tableau made it feel as if someone had cracked his heart wide open and stomped on it.

Marina had a child. With someone else.

He'd thought that he'd reached the depths of pain. Now he knew there was more—and it felt as if he were drowning. Someone else had the life he'd planned, the life he'd wanted: Marina, their baby, a fulfilling job.

Why the hell hadn't he tried harder to make it work?

Because he'd been an idiot.

Because he'd been hurting too much at the time to work out what he'd needed to do—what *they* had needed to do—as a couple.

And now it was too late. Way, way too late.

There was only one way of getting this out of his system. So, instead of making himself a sandwich when he got home, Max grabbed his gym gear and headed out again. What he needed was a workout that would leave him too damn tired to think. He'd sleep on it, let his subconscious come up with a way of dealing with the fact that Marina Petrelli was back in his life— and she was very firmly off-limits.

# CHAPTER TWO

THE roster fairy definitely wasn't on his side, Max thought the next morning as he walked into Resus and saw his team.

To think he'd been so cool and calm yesterday, asking Marina if it would be a problem for her, working in the same department. He'd been so sure that he could handle the situation.

Though, that had been before he'd seen her with her daughter.

And he was shocked by how much that thought still hurt, like a bruise that went right through his soul.

'Good morning, Dr Fenton,' Marina said.

She sounded bright and breezy, as if nothing was wrong—although he'd noticed that her smile didn't quite reach her eyes, and she was using his formal title rather than his first name.

OK; he'd take the lead from her. Bright, breezy and surface-friendly it was—even though he felt like punching something. He forced himself to unclench the fists in his pockets. 'Good morning, Dr Petrelli.'

'We've just had a shout,' she told him. 'RTC, elderly female passenger, ETA six minutes.'

'Any details?'

'Query fracture and internal injuries. They've put a line in and she's on a spinal board.'

Max met the ambulance crew at the door and quickly went through the handover, and the team swung into action to treat Mrs Jennings. Clearly they were used to working together and, whatever the problems between himself and Marina, she obviously took her job seriously, and she hadn't been exaggerating when she'd said that she could push the personal stuff into the background and put her patient first. Max quickly discovered that over the last four years Marina had become a fine doctor, confident and capable, and whenever he was about to give her some instructions he found she was already doing it, having second-guessed him.

As they assessed their patient for hypo-volaemic shock—Max wasn't happy with her blood pressure or the capillary refill—they both noted the pattern of bruising across her abdomen, the lap-belt imprint. On examination, Mrs Jennings' abdomen was tender. Not good.

'I'm not happy with this,' Max said quietly to Marina.

'I'd need to see the X-ray to confirm it, but my guess is that the impact fractured her pelvis,' Marina said, equally quietly.

He nodded. 'There may be some splenic in-volvement as well, or even damage to other organs. We need a CT scan and an X-ray to see what's going on.'

'Agreed. Let's get her stabilised first,' Marina said.

Quietly, Max asked Stella, their senior nurse, to bleep the orthopaedic-surgery team and put Theatre on standby, and then he turned back to the patient. 'Mrs Jennings, I'm going to put a mask over your face,' he said, 'to give you some oxygen, which will help you to breathe more easily. And I'm going to give you something to help with the pain, so it makes things a bit more comfortable for you while we take a look at your injuries. If you're worried about anything, just lift your hand and we'll take the mask off for a few moments so you can talk to us, OK?'

Mrs Jennings whispered her consent. Max fitted the oxygen mask over her face and gave her analgesia through the IV line that the paramedics had put in, while Marina inserted a second IV line and set up a drip. Marina took blood samples for rapid cross-matching, all the while talking to Mrs Jennings, reassuring her and assessing her. Max was impressed by Marina's calm, kind manner. Although they were faced with a potentially life-threatening emergency—compound pelvic fractures, especially if there were abdominal injuries as well, were associated with a mortality rate of more than fifty per cent—Marina made sure that Mrs Jennings didn't realise how worried they all were. She behaved as if this was a completely everyday occurrence, and nothing more worrying than a dislocated elbow, which meant that their patient relaxed rather than panicking—and in turn that made their investigations just that touch easier.

If it wasn't for the personal stuff between them, working with her would have been a dream.

As it was, it was a living nightmare. Her voice echoed through his head: *Let's go and meet Daddy. Daddy. Daddy.*

It should've been him.

He shook himself. This wasn't the time or the place. And there was nothing he could do to change the situation, so it was pointless ripping himself apart over it. He forced himself to stay in professional mode, and reviewed the X-rays with Marina against the lightbox. 'Classic open-book fracture,' he said.

'That's fixable. What worries me more is that her BP is still dropping.'

'Which means she has internal injuries.' He grimaced. 'We don't have time to wait for a CT scan, and even a DPL's going to be risky.' A diagnostic peritoneal lavage or DPL was a quick way of checking for internal haemorrhage when a scan would take too long. 'We need to get her up to Theatre now. Fast-bleep the orthopods, please, Stella,' he said to the nurse. 'I'm sending Mrs Jennings up.'

He turned to Mrs Jennings. 'The X-rays show that the accident broke your pelvis,' Max explained gently, holding her hand and looking into her eyes. 'I'm going to send you up to Theatre so the surgeons can fix it for you. We want to keep you as still as possible on the way, so we're going to put sandbags either side of you to make sure you don't move on the trolley.'

'But don't be afraid,' Marina added. 'It won't be uncomfortable, and it's pretty much routine-procedure for anyone who's got a break right there. I'm going to come up to Theatre with you and introduce you to the surgical team.' She took Mrs Jennings' other hand. 'And I'm not going to leave you until you're happy that you know what's going on. Is there anyone you'd like us to call for you while you're with the surgeons?'

Mrs Jennings reached up with her free hand and lowered the mask. 'My daughter,' she whispered.

Marina made a note of her name and number. 'I'll call her myself as soon as you're in Theatre,' she promised.

'And my friend,' Mrs Jennings whispered.

'The one who was driving me. Was she hurt in the accident?'

'She hasn't been brought in here,' Marina said. 'But I'll talk to the ambulance crew and find out what happened and how she is. Then, when you're out of Theatre, I'll come and see you and let you know what's going on. Now, let me put this mask back on you and make you more comfortable.'

When Marina returned from taking Mrs Jennings up to Theatre and phoning her daughter, Max was about to send her on a break, then the phone in Resus rang.

Stella answered it. 'Marina, it's the nursery,' she said, handing the phone to Marina.

'Marina Petrelli speaking.'

Even though Max tried hard not to listen in, he couldn't help noticing that Marina went white.

'What's happened? Right. I see. Yes, of course.' She replaced the receiver and blew out a breath. 'Phoebe's just thrown up everywhere. The nursery needs me to collect her and take her home, as in *right now*.' She bit her lip. 'Dr Fenton, I know I'm rostered in here with you today, and we're short-staffed, but—'

'Just go,' Max cut in. 'The child obviously needs you.' He couldn't bring himself to say 'your daughter'; the words made his throat feel as if it were closing, and he was angry with himself for not being able to get a grip. He should be happy that Marina's life was on track and that she'd clearly found a partner who loved her the way she deserved to be loved. The fact that he hadn't moved on and found someone else himself was his own stupid fault, and it wasn't fair to blame her for his own shortcomings. 'I'll arrange cover.'

'Thank you.' This time, her smile was genuine, gratitude, clearly mixed with fear for her child; she looked worried sick. And for good reason; he'd been told that the previous month the hospital had had to put a ban on visitors because so many patients and staff had been struck down by the winter vomiting-virus.

He didn't have time to add that he hoped it was nothing serious, because Marina had already left, walking very quickly, the way junior doctors soon learned to do so they could cover the ground between the on-call room and a department at maximum speed and with minimum risk.

To his surprise, Marina was back in the department again within two hours.

What the hell was she doing here? Her daughter was ill and needed her, and yet Marina was at work. Her priorities were *way* out of line. 'Shouldn't you be at home?' he demanded.

Marina shook her head. 'It's OK. Mum's taken over. I rang her on the way to collect Phoebe.'

'Your mother's looking after Phoebe?' He stared at her in disbelief. Just what was going on here? He knew that family was important to Marina, and given the way she'd fallen apart when she'd lost their baby he would've bet good money that she would always put her child before her job—before anything else. How could she just dump her sick daughter on her mother's doorstep?

Then again, the cost of living was high in London. Perhaps she and her partner were struggling financially and needed her salary to survive—what was left of it, after the cost of childcare.

'What about the child's father?' The question was out before he could stop it.

She looked defensive. 'Neil's really busy at work. I can't expect him to drop everything. Not when—'

'Save it. It's none of my business,' he cut in. He knew he was being rude, but he was angry—with himself, as much as with her. Why couldn't he get his head round the fact that Marina had moved on, that she'd found happiness with someone else? Why was he so selfish that he couldn't be pleased for her, or relieved that she wasn't stuck in the same limbo of misery that he was?

She said nothing, but her face looked pinched, and her dark eyes were wary whenever she spoke to him for the rest of the afternoon.

As Max's anger faded, he realised how just unfair he'd been. Which was why he sent Marina off the ward at five o'clock sharp.

'I can't leave when we still have a patient to treat,' she said in a low voice.

'We'll manage without you.'

'But—'

'Phoebe needs you. Go home.'

'But—'

'Go *home*,' he repeated, trying to make his voice gentle. It was obvious that Marina was torn between her child and her duty; he had no intention of making the choice any more difficult for her.

But he thought about it for the rest of the evening—and wondered. Had their child been ill, how would he have acted? He was pretty sure he knew—and his choice wouldn't have been the same as Neil's.

Then again, he hadn't exactly been a perfect husband to Marina. He hadn't been there when she'd needed him. Yes, work had been busy, but he'd used his career as an excuse to avoid facing the misery at home. He hadn't known how to make things better, for either of them, so he'd put his job first. Her second husband was clearly out of the same mould, so Max knew he was hardly in a position to criticise the guy. It didn't stop him feeling angry about the situation, though, or thinking that Marina deserved better.

\* \* \*

Wednesday; thank God it was Wednesday, Marina thought. As part of her training as a specialist registrar in emergency paediatrics, her boss had arranged for her to spend one day a week in the Children's Assessment Unit. She was covering in part for Katrina Morgan, who was on maternity leave. Rhys Morgan—the consultant, who was also Katrina's husband—had taught her a huge amount.

Marina loved every second of the time she spent on the CAU and always looked forward to it, but the fact that she didn't have to face Max today made it even better.

'Are you OK, Marina?' Rhys asked. 'You look a bit pale.'

'I'm fine,' Marina fibbed with a smile. 'Just tired.' She hadn't slept particularly well the previous night, brooding about Max and how hostile he'd been towards her. Yes, she'd been the one to walk out—but they were both equally responsible for the collapse of their marriage. And hadn't they agreed that they were going to put their patients first? If he carried on like that, there was no way they'd be able to work together—and it wouldn't be fair on their patients or the rest of the team.

'Not studying too hard, I hope?' Rhys said.

'No, just worrying about my sister.' It was true: just not the *whole* truth. Not that she was going to burden Rhys with the mess of her personal life. 'And, yes, I know she's in good hands and Theo Petrakis is the best maternity specialist for miles.' Theo's wife Madison and Rhys's wife Katrina were cousins, but were as close as sisters—though Marina knew that Rhys would have put the family connection aside when he'd assessed his colleague's medical skills, just as she would have.

'But Rosie's still your sister—and where your own family's concerned all your medical knowledge goes out of the window. You end up being like a medical student again, poring through textbooks and convincing yourself that you can see the symptoms of really rare complications,' Rhys said, smiling back. 'Katrina says I'm going to be a nightmare when she goes into labour, just as Theo was with Maddie.'

'Doctors, eh?' Marina said wryly. 'How is Katrina, by the way?'

'Blooming,' Rhys said. 'It's our first anniversary next week. I had planned to take her to Venice for the weekend, but with her being seven-and-a-half months' pregnant I don't want her to fly. So instead we're going to Southwold, on the coast of Suffolk.' He grinned. 'And, yes, I know that this cold snap means that the east coast is going to feel like Siberia. We'll just have to tough it out and snuggle up in front of a proper log-fire in the little thatched cottage I booked.'

'That sounds lovely. Really romantic,' Marina said, trying to keep the wistful note out of her voice. Rhys was deeply in love with his wife and had planned something special to celebrate their first anniversary, whereas she and Max hadn't even made it to their first anniversary.

They hadn't even made it to six months before their marriage had imploded.

And now he was back in her life, and all her feelings were turned upside down again. Anger, hurt, longing, love and hate, all shaken together so thoroughly that she couldn't work out which was which.

She pushed the thought aside. 'Righty. What do you have for me this morning?'

'Severe asthma—cold-induced. Several cases, actually.'

'And if it isn't brought back under control properly they could end up with silent chest—in which case they'll be downstairs with my lot,' Marina said. With asthma, the child's airways were inflamed, and responded rapidly and strongly to stimuli, so the child wheezed and coughed; the airways narrowed so much that the child couldn't breathe out properly. The child might then panic and the situation could spiral. If it got really out of control, the wheezing could stop, which was far more dangerous. 'Silent chest', as it was known, meant that the asthmatic patient wasn't moving enough air through their lungs to even create a wheeze—and that was life-threatening.

'And then, once you've stabilised them, back up with me for admission and overnight observation...' Rhys began.

'Because if there's a history of severe attacks there's a very good chance that a child who's had an attack during the day will have another one at night,' Marina finished.

'Exactly,' Rhys said. 'So part of today is going to be about prevention—talking to the parents about using their inhalers properly, how to use them and when. And it's worth making the point that the steroids we give aren't the same as body-building steroids—these are the ones that are produced naturally in the body.'

Marina nodded. 'And we'll make a note for the GP and health visitor.'

Rhys smiled. 'Working with you is almost like working with Katrina—she's spot on about kids, too. You know, I'm looking for someone to cover her maternity leave properly. Working up here for a while would be really good for your career development.'

Marina shook her head. 'Ellen agreed to let me work here for a day a week. I'm not sure she'd go for a year's secondment.'

'I can talk to her, if you like? Think about it,' Rhys said. 'The offer's open for a couple of weeks.'

'Thanks.' It was good to know that she had a potential bolthole. Working with Max and dealing with all the memories would've been tough at the best of times but, coming on top of her worries about Rosie and the baby, it just ratcheted up the tension.

At least here in the CAU she could relax.

And she could try not to think of Max.

# CHAPTER THREE

ON THURSDAY morning, Max was walking into the department when he heard Kelly on Reception say, 'Hey, Marina! How's Phoebe doing?'

'She's on the mend. It's just a tummy bug.' Marina smiled. 'That's the worst thing about being a medic—you know the worst-case scenarios, and instead of seeing a simple tummy bug you imagine it's the winter vomiting virus and all the complications that go with it.'

Max knew exactly what she meant, though sometimes medics went the other way, going into complete denial when faced with the evidence—just as they had done four years ago. They'd managed to convince themselves that Marina wasn't having a miscarriage, that the baby they hadn't planned but had both wanted so much would be just fine… And when they'd finally had to face the truth it had hurt even more.

'Though Rosie's pretty upset that she's not getting her usual visitor on the ward this morning. I rang her at breakfast, so Phoebe could say hello down the phone, but it's not the same as being able to cuddle her.'

Max knew he really shouldn't be listening in—it was nothing to do with him any more—but he'd always liked Marina's elder sister. Unless Rosie had changed career and become a medic like Marina, it sounded as if something was wrong. Why would Rosie be in hospital? And why was Marina taking her daughter to visit her sick aunt every single day?

'How's Rosie doing this morning?' Kelly asked.

'She's fine. Missing Phoebe and Neil like crazy, of course, but everyone knows she won't stick to bed rest at home.' Marina spread her hands. 'I mean, you can't if you have a toddler as lively as Phoebe.' She laughed. 'Mum's always telling Phoebe that she's exactly like her Aunty Rina was at the same age—covered in glitter and paint half the time, and pedalling round on her tricycle the other half.'

Everything suddenly fell into place for Max, and for one crazy moment he found himself on the point of whooping with delight and doing a happy dance all round the department.

The toddler Marina had been carrying—the one she'd gone to pick up from the nursery—was her *niece*, not her daughter.

As Rosie had the same colouring as Marina, and similar features, of course there'd be a strong physical resemblance between aunt and niece. And that in turn meant that the man Marina had kissed in the corridor had been her brother-in-law, not her partner. The Petrelli family had always been warm and tactile, and Max had kissed Marina's sister, mother, aunts and grand-mother exactly the same way himself before their marriage had fallen apart.

How *stupid* he'd been.

Then again, Max had never been able to think straight around Marina. Not from the moment he'd met her as a wet-behind-the-ears junior doctor who made very sure she pulled her weight on the team and did her best to reassure her patients. They'd gone for a coffee after that first shift, and had dated every night after that. The more time he'd spent with her, the more deeply he'd fallen in love with her.

Small wonder that they'd gone to bed together within a week and had moved in together within a month. They hadn't wanted to spend a single moment apart.

Yet they'd spent the past four years as far apart as they could be: Marina in London, and he moving from disaster zone to disaster zone, pushing himself to the limit so he wouldn't have to think about how much he'd lost.

He closed his eyes briefly. Now wasn't the time or the place. He and Marina were going to have to talk about it, but not now, and definitely not here. Right now, he had a job to do. And so did she.

Marina was rostered on the children's section of the emergency department that morning; that was good, because it meant she didn't have to see Max. Not unless there was a really difficult case where she needed a second opinion. But she was in luck: her first case was a toddler who'd stuffed a plastic bead up her nose, her second was a child with a cough that she suspected was asthmatic, and her third was one who'd fallen in the playground and gashed his arm deeply enough to need stitches and a lot of reassurance. All things that needed a bit of time, reassurance and TLC as well as medical treatment, and she knew she was perfectly capable of dealing with all of them on her own.

Everything was fine until she took her break. The second that she made herself a mug of coffee in the kitchen, Max walked in, as if he had some weird kind of radar that told him exactly when she'd be there.

'How's Phoebe?' he asked.

'Doing OK, thanks. Mum's looking after her today again.'

He made himself a coffee, then took a bar of chocolate from the pocket of his white coat, snapped it in half and handed half to her.

She accepted it without thinking, the way she always had when they'd worked together.

'Thanks.' Then she stared at the chocolate, suddenly realising what they'd both done.

*Just like old times.*

Except they'd both come a long way in the last four years.

'I didn't have time for breakfast this morning,' he said with the quirky smile that had once made her knees melt.

She remembered those days. Even though their flat had been a ten-minute walk from the hospital, they'd never had time for breakfast. Because they'd been too busy making love.

She took a gulp of coffee and willed the memories to stay back.

'So what's wrong with Rosie?' he asked. 'I overheard Kelly asking you how she was.'

'Pre-eclampsia,' Marina explained. 'They've kept her in so she'll get some rest and they can monitor how the baby's doing.'

'Is it OK if I go and see her?' he asked.

She frowned. 'Why would you want to do that?'

He sighed. 'Look, I know things didn't work out between us, but I liked your family.'

And they'd liked him. A lot.

Pity that the same couldn't be said of the way Max's family had felt about her. Kay Fenton had seen Marina as a rival for her son's affections, and Andrew Fenton had usually been away on business trips. Marina had found them distant and cold, the complete opposite of her own family. And when everything had gone wrong, and Marina had been at her most vulnerable, the Fentons had made it very clear that they weren't going to offer her a shoulder to cry on. Andrew, as usual, had been absent, and Kay had actually said that it was for the best—that it was the wrong time for Max to have a baby when he had his career to think about.

How could anyone possibly say that a miscarriage was 'for the best'? All this time later, it still took her breath away.

'Marina?'

It wasn't Max's fault that his mother was supremely tactless. 'It's not up to me to give you permission. If you want to visit Rosie—' she spread her hands '—then visit her. But bear in mind she has pre-eclampsia. The last thing she needs right now is any kind of worry that'll make her blood pressure rise.'

'As a medic, I'd just about worked that one out for myself,' Max said drily.

'Sorry. I didn't mean to be rude.' She blew out a breath. 'It's just…'

'She's your big sister, you love her and you worry about her,' Max supplied.

'Yes.'

'It's good that she has family who care.'

Marina was careful not to comment, and she took refuge in eating the chocolate he'd given her.

He sighed. 'Look, if you're worrying—nobody here knows about Bristol. And I'm happy for it to stay that way. I don't like being gossiped about, either. If anyone twigs that we know each other, we'll just tell them we worked together years ago and lost touch.'

It was the truth. Just not the whole truth. And it left out a hell of a lot of pain in between. 'Thank you,' she said quietly.

He looked away. 'We have to work together, and there's enough tension in an emergency department as it is without adding to it.'

'Agreed.'

'So can we just drop the formality and treat each other like any other member of staff?'

'Sure.' But he wasn't just 'any other member of staff'. He never could be. But Marina had already been there, done that and had her heart well and truly broken. She wasn't going to take that risk a second time. No matter that she still found Max incredibly attractive physically; she knew that they weren't compatible. And, although part of her would've been more than happy to walk back into his arms, part of her knew that it'd be a huge mistake. She'd simply be setting herself up for more misery. So she was going to have to learn to think of him as just a colleague.

Somehow.

She drained her coffee. 'I'd better get back. Thanks for the chocolate.'

'Pleasure.'

During his lunch break, Max called in at the hospital shop to buy chocolates and a puzzle magazine—he'd already learned that the hospital had a clear-locker-top policy, and flowers were discouraged, to help in the battle with hygiene—and went up to the maternity ward.

'We have protected lunchtimes, I'm afraid,'

the senior midwife told him firmly. 'Sorry. You'll have to come back later.'

'Is there any chance you can bend the rules for me, as staff?' Max asked. 'I promise to be quiet. And I have a feeling that this particular patient hates being on bed rest. So that's fifteen minutes or so when you won't have to keep an eye on her and nag her, because I can do it for you.'

She glanced at his name-tag. 'Ah. You work with Rosie's sister?'

'I do indeed.' Max had no intention of giving the more complicated explanation—that Rosie was his ex-sister-in-law. He held out his free hand. 'Max Fenton, emergency senior registrar.'

She shook his hand and introduced herself. 'Iris Rutherford, senior midwife. No doubt we'll be working together at some point.'

'Good to meet you outside of a crisis.' Max gave her his most charming smile.

'All right. You can have fifteen minutes,' Iris said. 'But you'd better make sure she rests and doesn't move, or I'll be forced to scalp you.'

He laughed, enjoying her direct approach. 'I will. Thank you, Iris.'

Max followed her directions; Rosie was in a room on her own, flicking listlessly through a magazine and looking very fed up.

'Psst. Open for visitors?' he asked from the doorway.

She looked at him, and then gave him a broad smile. 'Max Fenton! What on earth are you doing here?'

'Visiting you,' he said, walking into the room and closing the door behind him.

Her eyes widened. 'We're not allowed visitors at lunchtime.'

'I know.' He laughed. 'I begged.'

'Charmed, more like. You always could melt women's knees with that gorgeous smile of yours.' She grinned and held her arms open. 'Come and give me a hug, Max. It's good to see you.'

'And it's good to see you, Rosie Petrelli.' And even better to be hugged like that again. He'd missed the warmth of Marina's family, and his own. Well…he'd always found his mother's hugs stifling rather than warm. Though, now that everything was finally out in the open about his father, he could understand the way she behaved. Could sympathise, even.

'I'm Rosie Brown nowadays.' She bit her lip. 'I'm sorry I didn't invite you to the wedding, Max. But, apart from the fact that you'd cut off all contact with us, it would've been a bit—'

'Awkward, given who was probably your chief bridesmaid,' he finished wryly, sitting on the chair next to her bed. 'You did the right thing. I would've brought you some flowers, but I gather they've been banned from the hospital for a while. I hope these will do.' He placed the goodies on her lap.

'My favourites; you remembered I love white chocolate.' She beamed at him. 'And you managed to find the only puzzle magazine I haven't already gone through. Thank you. That's so, so sweet of you, *caro*.'

'My pleasure. So how long have you been in here?'

'Nineteen days, and counting,' Rosie said with a rueful smile, 'thanks to my bossy little sister.'

'Marina picked it up?' Max looked at her, surprised.

'She was on a day off, so she came to have

lunch with me. I wasn't feeling brilliant; I thought it was just a bit of indigestion and a headache. But when I told her where the pain was she wasn't happy about it. She said it was rare to get pre-eclampsia with a second baby, but she wanted it checked out. She made me call the midwife and then drink loads of water.'

Ready for a urine test, no doubt. Rosie wasn't in the high-risk group, though: she was under thirty-five, her weight was average and it wasn't her first pregnancy. As far as Max knew, there wasn't a family history of pre-eclampsia, and Rosie wasn't a diabetic. Plus, from what Marina had said, she was only expecting one baby, not twins or triplets. 'So where was the pain? Just under your ribs?'

Rosie rolled her eyes. 'Spoken just like a doctor! Yes. And, yes, before you ask, there turned out to be a little bit of protein in my urine and my blood pressure was a bit on the high side.'

Knowing Rosie, that was a major understatement.

'So they're keeping me in to monitor the baby and keep an eye on me,' she finished.

'How far are you?'

'Thirty-three weeks—and it's driving me insane, being stuck here.' She shook herself. 'And here's me being ungrateful. Marina's been absolutely brilliant. And, yes, I do know she probably saved my life.'

If Rosie's symptoms hadn't been picked up so quickly, she could have been very ill—and there would've been a serious risk both to the baby and to Rosie herself. If Rosie's condition had turned into eclampsia, both of them could have died.

'She's sorted out a place at the hospital crèche for Phoebe while I'm here, and she brings my baby in to see me every morning before her shift. She picks her up, too, if she's on an early. Neil's boss has been really good about him working more flexible hours, but it's smack in the middle of the busy season.'

'Busy season?'

'It's March—coming up to the end of the tax year. He's an accountant,' Rosie explained, 'so normally he'd be working silly hours in the office, but because I'm stuck in here he's having to bring work home and do it when Phoebe's asleep. Mum and Dad have been brilliant, too. Dad's painting the baby's room and Mum's keeping the house ticking over and making sure that there's food in the fridge, so Neil can spend time here with me and Phoebe instead of worrying about housework and shopping and what have you.'

Exactly what Max would expect from the Petrellis, being there to help with practical things in a crisis. Part of him wondered: had he and Marina lived in London instead of Bristol, would her family have rallied round them and kept them together, helped them to work things through?

Too late for that now.

'So when are they going to induce you?' he asked.

'It depends how things go. I know that it's best to deliver the baby as late as possible, but the idea of being stuck here for another seven weeks, having injections and blood taken…' She grimaced. 'I tell you, if I was ever scared of needles, I've learned to overcome my phobia! Anyway, enough about me. We're doing fine—

aren't we, Bambino?' She rubbed the bump and smiled. 'So, how are you doing?'

'I'm fine.'

She raised an eyebrow. 'Right. And that's why you've got dark shadows under your eyes and you're too thin. Don't try to bluff me, Max.'

'New city, new job. It takes time to settle in,' he said lightly.

'Maybe.' She gestured to his name-tag. 'But you're also working in the emergency department with my sister. That can't be easy—for either of you.'

He shrugged. 'We're professionals. Our patients won't suffer.'

'I'm not talking about the *patients*—I know you're both professionals. I was talking about you two.' She reached out and took his hand. 'I was really sorry when you and Marina broke up.'

*Tell me about it.* He forced himself to keep the words back. 'Things happen,' he said lightly.

'So are you with someone now? What's she like?'

He'd forgotten the other thing about Marina's family: they had no scruples about asking personal questions. For a moment, he considered making up a story, but Rosie would know he was lying. 'There's nobody,' he admitted. And then, to stave off further questioning, he added, 'I spent a few years working for Doctors Without Borders. There wasn't time for anything other than work.'

He wished he hadn't said it when Rosie gave him a very perceptive look. 'So *that's* why we never got a Christmas card from you. Hmm. I happen to know someone else who throws herself into work. Someone who either finds excuses not to date, or makes it friends-only after just a couple of dates.'

Rosie wasn't even trying to be subtle and, although part of him was annoyed, part of him was also amused. The Petrellis were notorious fixers. They were the kind of people who made lemonade out of lemons, who always saw the bright side. It was one of the things he'd adored about Marina; she was unlike anyone else he'd ever met. And the complete opposite of his mother: she saw sunshine where Kay Fenton saw clouds, was light where Kay was intense.

Just like the rest of her family. 'Don't get your hopes up, Rosie. Marina and I are colleagues. End of.' He smiled to take the sting from his words.

'It's four years now since you split up. You're both still single. That,' Rosie said, 'is extremely telling.'

'And I think you've been teaching too much *Romeo and Juliet*,' he said, still managing a smile. It was impossible to be offended with someone who so clearly wanted life to be happy. 'A nice story.'

She scoffed. 'Of course it isn't a nice story. It's a tragedy, Max. They both die at the end!'

'And it unites their families.' He flapped a dismissive hand. 'You know what I mean. Marina and I won't be getting back together, Rosie. There's way too much water under the bridge.'

Rosie gave him a telling look, but to his relief she didn't try to labour the point. 'Marina didn't tell me you were working here.'

He shrugged. 'I only started a couple of days ago.'

'Hmm,' Rosie said.

'And neither of us knew the other was working here. It was a bit of a surprise for both of us.'

'I'll say,' Rosie said drily.

He ruffled her hair. 'I have to go. Iris says you have to sit still and be good, or she'll scalp me. Is it OK if I come back tomorrow?'

'Of course it is.' She frowned. 'Why are you even asking me that?'

'I don't want to make things awkward.'

'With Marina, you mean? Or the rest of my family?' She patted his hand. 'Stop worrying. Of course it's not going to be awkward. If anything, they'll be pleased I've got someone else to come in and nag me to rest.'

He couldn't help laughing. 'Good.'

She smiled at him. 'Thanks for coming, Max. It's been really good to see you again.'

'You, too.' He hugged her, and left for the emergency department.

But he couldn't stop thinking about what Rosie had told him.

*Marina didn't date.*

He hadn't dated much since he'd split up with

Marina, either. Most of the time, he'd been too busy at work to bother with a relationship. But when he'd come back to England and had started dating again something had always been missing. He'd always ended up finishing a relationship before it had even got started.

If he was honest with himself, he knew why: because nobody had ever matched up to his ex-wife.

And Rosie had told him that there was nobody serious in Marina's life, either.

Quite what that meant, he didn't know. Did Marina still have feelings for him? But, in that case, surely she would've talked to him and asked him to give their marriage another try, instead of sending divorce papers to him? Or maybe marriage to him had disappointed her so much that she wasn't prepared to try again with anyone else.

The only way to find out was to ask her.

Though, it wasn't the easiest of subjects to broach. Particularly as they had to work together. Right now, they had a guarded working-relationship; not an easy one, but a tolerable one. Asking the wrong questions at the wrong time could tip it over into being intolerable—which wouldn't be fair to their colleagues.

Last time, they'd rushed into things, and it had gone spectacularly wrong. This time, maybe he should try being patient.

And when the time was right, Max decided, then he'd ask those questions.

# CHAPTER FOUR

Over the next week, Marina found herself growing more and more aware of her ex. She knew exactly when Max walked into the department, even if she was busy treating a patient in cubicles and couldn't see him. And, when they were working together in Resus, she was conscious of every single movement he made. Time and again she found herself glancing at him, only to find that he was looking at her too.

This was insane. They'd crashed and burned last time round. So why couldn't they keep their eyes off each other?

Every time his hand brushed hers as she handed him an ampoule, or he passed her a syringe, or they looked at an X-ray together, her pulse started racing—because her body still remembered the way he used to touch her: the feel of his skin sliding against hers, the roughness of the hair on his chest, the softness of his mouth as he'd kissed her awake. The scent of his skin, the way his eyes crinkled at the corners and dimples appeared in his cheeks when he laughed, the way desire flared in his eyes and turned them from slate-blue to hot black whenever he looked at her.

She really had to get a grip. If this carried on for much longer, she'd go crazy.

She and Max were *not* an item. They were never going to be an item again. And it was about time her head got that straight.

Rosemary; Max would've known that scent anywhere. So Marina still used the same shampoo, then.

Her hair was driving him insane. She wore it in a French pleat at work, but he could remember what it looked like when it was down, glossy and spilling over her shoulders. Flowing over his pillow, soft and sensuous. He'd loved brushing her hair, playing with the ends and feeling its silkiness against his skin.

It would have been so much easier if she'd had

her hair cropped. At least then he wouldn't have had to keep battling with the memories.

He glanced at her mouth, and wished that he hadn't. Because he could remember that beautiful mouth exploring every inch of his skin, her eyes full of mischief as she'd turned him on so much that he couldn't even see straight. Even the memories made his whole body tingle with desire.

Working with Marina was becoming more and more of a challenge for Max. She was a great doctor, and he'd never been one for throwing his weight around, so teamwork on the ward wasn't a problem.

It was Marina herself, and the way his body seemed to operate completely independently from his head. Every time his hand accidentally brushed hers, or he caught the scent of her hair, he wanted to yank her into his arms, dip his head, brush his mouth against hers, tease her until she slid her hands into his hair, opened her mouth and kissed him back.

For pity's sake. He knew he didn't have the right to do that. But he still wanted to touch her. *Needed* to touch her.

This was crazy, particularly as he didn't have a clue how she felt about the situation. She was perfectly professional with him, and since their brief chat in the staff kitchen she'd stuck to first-name terms and treated him just like she treated everyone else on the ward. But whenever he caught her eye there was something unreadable in her gaze. He couldn't even begin to work out what it was.

*Get a grip*, he told himself savagely. *Be professional.* Because he knew it was way too late to go back. No way would Marina give him a second chance.

'Max has been to see me,' Rosie said.

Marina frowned. 'He hasn't upset you or anything, has he?'

'No. He's good company. And he's dropped in every day.'

Every day? From what he'd said, she'd expected him to visit Rosie maybe once—not every day. And he hadn't said a word to her about it.

Rosie took her sister's hand and squeezed it. 'I always liked him, Marina. We all did.'

'I know.' Marina sighed heavily, guessing what Rosie was going to say next, and knowing that she had to head her sister off right now. 'But it didn't work out and we've both moved on.'

'Mmm-hmm.' Rosie paused. 'You know, Max isn't seeing anyone.'

'That's none of my business, Rosie.' Trust her sister to have asked the question. Marina deliberately hadn't.

But now she knew.

And it sent a weird mixture of delight and panic through her.

Delight, because it felt as if Max had waited for her. And panic, because it had gone so badly wrong last time; did they really have a chance to get it right, second time round?

If Max had wanted them to try again, he would have followed her to London years ago. He would've refused to sign the divorce papers. He would've *talked* to her.

But, all the same, she couldn't help wondering: why was Max still single? OK, so their marriage had been a disaster, but Max was a nice guy. A good doctor.

*A thoughtful lover.* Marina suppressed that line of thought immediately. She really didn't need to remember how she'd felt in Max's arms. How his clever hands and mouth had made her blood feel, as if it were singing. How he'd taken her to the edge of pleasure.

'Did you know he spent three years working for Doctors Without Borders?' Rosie asked.

'No.' But it explained why he'd taken a while to respond to her solicitor's letters—and it also explained why he was single. No way would Max have had any spare energy to start a new relationship, working under those kinds of pressures.

'I think,' Rosie said, 'that it's time you two sat down and talked. Properly.'

Ha. That had been one of the biggest blows to their marriage. After she'd lost the baby, they'd stopped talking. 'There isn't anything to say.'

'Isn't there?' Rosie arched one eyebrow.

'No. Now, stop worrying.' Marina patted her hand. 'As I said, we've both moved on.'

Rosie folded her arms. 'Right. Which is why neither of you are dating.'

'If he's been working for Doctors Without

Borders, he wouldn't have had time to see anyone,' Marina pointed out. 'And I'm training to be a specialist registrar in paediatric emergency—which means I don't have time to see anyone either.' She gave her sister her brightest smile. 'Right now, my career needs to come first.'

'I worry about you, Marina. I want you to be happy.'

'I *am* happy.' Though, even as she said it, Marina realised it wasn't strictly true. She still missed Max. Or maybe she missed the idea of him: the man she'd thought she'd married, who'd turned out to be not quite the same as the man she'd actually married. 'Stop fussing and let me look at your chart,' she said to put Rosie off the scent.

Rosie groaned. 'They hate you doing that, you know.'

Marina laughed. 'No, they don't. Iris knows that I'm not going to interfere with the way they're looking after you. And this saves her some precious time—she doesn't have to spend ages with me while I grill her about how you *really* are.' She took the clipboard from the holder next to her sister's bed. 'Good. Your temperature's fine, your urine's fine… Hmm; your blood pressure's still not what I'd like it to be, but it's holding. And Bambino here seems to be doing very nicely, thank you. Excellent.'

'I've been here for ever and ever,' Rosie complained. 'I want to go home and play with my little girl.'

'I know you miss her, but she'll be here in a minute.' Marina gave her sister a hug. 'Hang on in there, sis. You're doing brilliantly.'

As if perfectly on cue, their mother walked in, holding Phoebe's hand.

'Mummy!'

Louise Petrelli lifted her granddaughter so Phoebe could sit next to her mother, and Rosie enfolded her in a hug, holding her tightly and pressing her face to the little girl's hair so she could breathe in her scent.

If things had been different, Marina would've met her baby from school with that same mother-daughter hug. The one that said how much they'd missed each other, even though both had been happily busy all day. The one that said how glad they were to be together again.

She envied Rosie that closeness. Funny; she thought she'd cried herself out over the miscarriage. But even now she was still yearning. Still wishing things had been different. Still not really over it.

Whereas Max… She had no idea how he'd felt about it, back then, and even less idea as to whether he still thought of their baby that might have been. He hadn't broken down the way she had—which didn't mean that he'd felt nothing—but he'd pushed her away, hadn't let her comfort him. Hadn't given her the support she'd needed so desperately.

Pushing the thoughts away, she gave her own mother a hug. 'Hi, Mum. Have you both had a good day?'

'Brilliant. We went to the park this morning and played on the swings, and this afternoon we've been busy making cookies, and pictures with glitter and glue—oh, and singing songs.'

Just the kind of thing that Marina remembered doing in her own childhood. The Petrelli household had been noisy, chaotic and messy, and chock-full of love. There had always been a tin full of fresh-baked cookies or cupcakes in the kitchen, and all the neighbours had seemed to congregate at their house. The mums would be round Louise's kitchen table with mugs full of good coffee, and the children would be playing noisy, messy games in the huge conservatory that opened off the kitchen, far enough away to feel independent, and yet near enough to be scooped up and kissed better within seconds if they fell over.

Completely the opposite of Max's family home, where nothing was ever out of place and the silence was practically deafening. She'd just bet that Max had never been allowed to do anything with glitter, and there wouldn't have been a cork board in his mother's kitchen where his newest paintings from school had been pinned up—because a cork board would have looked so out of place and scruffy in Kay Fenton's immaculate designer-kitchen.

'Sounds like fun,' Rosie said, looking as wistful as Marina felt.

'Hey, Mum, guess who's been visiting me this week?' Rosie asked.

Uh-oh. Marina had hoped that the delight of seeing her daughter would push the subject out of her sister's mind. Now she'd have two of them on her case.

'Who?' Louise asked.

'Max. *Marina's* Max.'

'Oh, really?' Louise looked intrigued.

'He's not *my* anything. We just work together.' Marina rolled her eyes. 'Mum, don't listen to her. She's bored and making up stories to amuse herself.'

'I am not,' Rosie said indignantly.

Phoebe snuggled into her mother. 'Story?' she asked hopefully.

Marina took the chance to escape before her mother could grill her any more, but she knew that the reckoning was only being delayed.

And, just as she'd expected, her mother phoned later that evening. 'So, what's the real story about Max?' Louise asked.

'There isn't one. He joined the team last week, so we're working together. We're both professional enough to put our patients first, so it isn't a problem.'

'Hmm.' Louise sounded as suspicious as Rosie had. 'Are you sure you're OK about this?'

'Really, Mum, there's nothing to worry about. It's fine.'

Louise sighed. 'All right. I won't nag. Your sister can do enough of that for both of us. But if it gets tough you know where I am.'

'I know, and I appreciate it,' Marina said, meaning every word. 'I love you, Mum.'

'Max, we're one short for Friday night,' Eve told him. 'Are you busy?'

'One short for what?' he asked.

'Ten-pin bowling.'

He smiled. 'Thanks for asking, Eve, but I haven't done that for years. I'd just let the side down.'

'Of course you wouldn't. Now's your chance to brush up your skills. And it's a good way of getting to know people outside work.'

Max had already worked out that Eve was the sort of person who took new members of the team under her wing and made sure that they felt welcome. And he knew that Marina was off duty on Friday, so it was highly likely that she wouldn't be there—she was bound to be doing something with her family. So Max judged that it was pretty safe to agree. 'Sure. Just let me know where and what time you want me to turn up.'

'Brilliant.' She gave him a broad smile. 'You won't regret it.'

Though he did regret it, the moment that he walked into the bowling alley and saw the group of people there.

Seeing Marina in a white coat was one thing. Seeing her in figure-hugging jeans and a loose, long-sleeved T-shirt with her hair down was quite another. At work, she was professional and detached; here, she looked like the girl next door. Just like she'd looked when she'd been his wife.

Five years ago, he would have strode over to her, swept her off her feet, spun her round and kissed her lingeringly, not caring who was watching. Five years ago, she'd have been sitting on his lap, laughing with him and stealing kisses while they were waiting for their respective turns at the bowling alley.

But this was now.

And, with the emotional distance between them, she might just as well have been standing on the moon.

He shoved his hands into the pockets of his jeans, just in case he was tempted to reach out and smooth his palm over the curve of her bottom. For pity's sake. He'd told himself this enough times; he knew he didn't have the right to touch her any more. The fact that he wanted to yank her into his arms and kiss her until they were both breathless and had forgotten the rest of the world…

They really needed to have that talk.

And it looked as if it had better be sooner rather than later.

'Sorry. I didn't realise you'd be here tonight, or I would've made some excuse and not come,' he said quietly as he joined the group.

She lifted one shoulder in a half-shrug. 'Nothing to apologise for—you're part of the team. You have as much right as I do to be here.'

She sounded all cool, calm and neutral—though he could see the tension in her face, in her mouth, and knew that she too was wishing herself thousands of miles away. This was as much of an ordeal for her as it was for him.

As luck would have it, they ended up on the same team of four. Max's turn to bowl was right after Marina's; short of standing with his back to her when she was bowling—which would've made it look way too obvious that he was trying to avoid her—there was nothing he could do but stand and watch her. The sight of the curve of her bottom, encased in soft, soft denim, sent his blood pressure up a notch, and he had to stuff his hands in his pockets to stop himself reaching out and touching her. Stroking her. She was still the most gorgeous woman he'd ever met, all softness and lush curves. He wanted her so badly, it was a physical pain. Worse, because he could remember how it felt when she touched him, could remember how it felt to lose himself inside her.

When their waiter brought cold drinks and hot, crispy nachos, Max's discomfort was magnified a hundred times, because he reached for the snacks at the same time as Marina and his fingers brushed against hers. It was the lightest, most casual touch, but every nerve-end in his body screamed into life. It felt as if his blood were fizzing through his veins.

He was extremely glad that his jeans were relatively baggy. The last thing he wanted was anyone noticing his arousal, or guessing his reaction to Marina—especially Marina herself.

Cool, calm and casual. That was how Marina had decided to play it tonight, when Max had turned up.

Except he *would* have to wear a T-shirt that brought out the slate-blue of his eyes. She'd fallen in love with his beautiful eyes all those years before, though she'd forgotten how long his lashes were. How he'd looked when he was asleep, like a fallen angel. Sexy as hell.

Yet there were also definite changes in him. She could see dark shadows underneath his eyes, and there was a kind of wariness and a reserve about him that she didn't remember from before, though maybe that was a result of his years working for Doctors Without Borders. She knew from talking to colleagues in her last hospital that the experience changed you.

But the thing that she really noticed was that Max looked...*unloved.*

It made her want to hold him close, tell him that everything would be OK because she was there, and she...

Oh, hell. She really had to stop thinking like this. It hadn't worked out last time; admittedly, they were both four years older and wiser now, but there was too much debris from the past for it to work out this time.

Though she couldn't deny that the attraction was still there between them. When their fingers had accidentally brushed each other's over the nachos, pure desire had rippled down her spine. And when she'd glanced at him he'd masked his expression quickly—but not before she'd noticed how huge his pupils were. Given how bright the lights were in the bowling alley, she had a pretty shrewd idea that Max was remembering the same kind of thing that she was.

Touching.

Tasting.

Losing themselves in each other.

They were really going to have to talk about this. But not at the hospital, and nowhere that they were likely to be spotted together or over-heard; the last thing she wanted was for them to become the hottest topic on the hospital grape-vine. She'd think about it over the weekend. Plan her strategy. And she'd tackle him on Monday.

# CHAPTER FIVE

EXCEPT on Monday there wasn't any time to think. Marina was working with Max in Resus, and there was a constant stream of cases—a woman with chest pain, a man with severe abdominal pain and an elderly man with a transient ischaemic attack. The team was working flat out, and they had just about enough time to grab half a sandwich before the next shout.

Max looked grim. 'We have a teenager on his way in. He was on his bike, not wearing a helmet; a car clipped him and he came off and hit his head. GCS 7.'

A Glasgow Coma Score of 7 meant that the boy was unconscious and unresponsive—and it was harder to judge his injuries. Given that he'd hit his head, his injuries could be severe. Life-threatening, even.

'Stella—can you warn radiology that we'll need an urgent CT scan, please, and get neurology on standby?' Max asked.

Moments after the handover, Marina could see that the neuro obs weren't good. She wasn't happy with the boy's pulse rate or his blood pressure, and even less happy that he still hadn't regained full consciousness twenty minutes after the accident.

'Witnesses say he was playing chicken, crossing the road on his bike between parked cars,' Max told her drily. 'Apparently the car driver tried to avoid him and did an emergency stop, but he didn't stand a chance.'

'The boy or the driver?'

'Both,' Max said. 'They're bringing the driver separately. He has whiplash—and he's pretty distressed.'

'Anyone would be, in his shoes.' She'd once accidentally backed into a car and broken her rear light, and that had been upsetting enough; when the collision hurt a person rather than a fixable object, even if it wasn't the driver's fault, it must be unbelievably frightening. 'What a mess,' Marina said.

Max swiftly intubated the boy and they set up ventilation. The boy's cervical spine was still protected by the board. 'I've got a bad feeling about this one,' Max said.

'Skull fracture?' Marina said.

Max nodded. 'And maybe a haematoma.' A blood clot that caused the brain to swell and pressure to rise within the cranium was a problem often caused with head injuries, and it could be fatal.

Max grimaced as he reviewed the CT scan. 'Look,' he said, pointing out the fracture at the base of the boy's skull. 'And here.' There were definite signs of a haematoma.

'Hurts,' the boy said, opening his eyes and closing them again almost straight away.

But at least he was talking; that was a good sign.

'Where does it hurt?' Marina asked.

The boy mumbled something neither of them could catch—and then was silent.

Marina and Max shared a glance. 'I hope this isn't a textbook case,' Max said.

She knew what he meant: 'talk and die'. They'd both seen cases like this before in Bristol, where a patient seemed to start recovering, said a few words—and then died just minutes later.

'His BP's rising,' Marina said.

'And he's bradycardic. Looks like a Cushing response to me.' Max's mouth tightened.

The Cushing response was when blood pressure rose and the heart rate fell; it meant there was increased intracranial pressure. Given the circumstances surrounding the boy's accident and what they'd seen on the CT scan, Marina knew Max thought the problem was caused by the haematoma getting bigger.

'I'll call the neuro team,' she said. A few moments later, she came back over to Max. 'The neurosurgeon says give him a bolus of mannitol—it'll buy time to get him upstairs to Theatre so they can drain the haematoma.'

But they both knew it might not be enough time.

Max administered the mannitol, and the boy was rushed upstairs to Theatre.

Although they were rushed off their feet for the rest of the afternoon, Marina knew that Max was thinking of the boy, just as she was. And the longer it went without any news the more worried she became. Neurosurgery was delicate and draining a haematoma took time, especially when a fracture was involved too, but surely they should have heard by now?

In the one break she managed to snatch between patients, she called her mother to say that it was frantic in the department and asked her to pick up Phoebe. So at the end of her shift, while Max was doing the handover, instead of rushing to the hospital crèche she called the neuro team to see if there was any news on their patient.

'I was on my way down to see you.' Fergus Keating, the neurosurgeon, sighed heavily. 'Sorry, Marina. We did what we could, but right when I thought we were on our way out of the woods we lost him on the table.'

'I'm sorry, too.' Brief, bare words, but she knew that Fergus understood what she meant: sympathy, because he'd tried his hardest, but the boy's injuries had been too severe for him to save the lad. And he also had the task of breaking the bad news to the boy's parents; giving bad news to the next of kin was one of the toughest parts of their job. 'I'll tell the others.'

'Thanks.'

She put the phone down and took a deep breath.

Max, who'd been doing the handover, noticed the pallor in Marina's face as she replaced the receiver.

'Marina?' he asked, going over to her.

She shook her head, as if unable to speak, and just walked out of Resus.

Max recognised the signs. Apart from the fact he'd seen this happen to colleagues a few times in his Doctors Without Borders days, he'd seen Marina crumble like this before. He also knew what it probably meant: that Marina had just been talking to the neurosurgeon and it was bad news.

He remembered that losing a patient had always hit Marina hard, and she'd always taken it personally. Four years' more experience in the emergency department clearly hadn't changed that. Her family was so good at fixing things that she simply couldn't deal with it on the rare occasions when it didn't happen—and it didn't matter that nobody else could've fixed things in the situation, either. In her view, she'd failed.

He followed her into the staff kitchen. She was halfway through filling a glass of water when she doubled over, shaking and not saying a word.

He put his arms round her, spun her round and held her close. 'It's OK,' he said softly. 'Talk to me. Let it out.'

She was still shaking, but clearly she was too upset for tears. 'He—he didn't make it,' she whispered.

Max had guessed as much.

'I hate losing patients, Max. I *hate* it when we can't save them.'

'We do our best, but we're only human. We can't save everyone. You know that.' He stroked her hair; he could smell the familiar scent of rosemary, and it felt so good to have her back in his arms. What kind of selfish pig was he, to be thinking of his own gratification and pleasure when she was upset? 'Marina, we did our best for him. So did the neuro team. Nobody could've done more.'

'I know.' She shuddered. 'But it always feels so much worse when we lose a child. It's bad enough when someone's old, but at least they've had a chance to live—a child has barely started living. And what about his family? There's going to be a huge hole in their lives. I mean, if he was playing chicken he was probably a difficult kid and hell to live with, but even so he was still their child. Losing…' She choked on the word.

'I know, honey.' He kept his arms round her, telling himself it was so she could draw strength and comfort from him, and knowing full well that he was taking just as much strength and comfort back from her.

But he really needed to make her feel better, and there was only one way he knew how.

'I'm pulling rank. Making an executive decision,' he said.

'What?' She looked at him, her dark eyes filled with incomprehension.

'At a time like this, the only thing that works is comfort food. Come on. We're both off duty, and I've done the handover.'

'Max, where are you…?'

'Taking you for some comfort food,' he repeated. 'And, before you ask, I'd do the same for anyone on my team.'

It wasn't a complete fib. He'd take an upset team member for a coffee and a sandwich and let them talk it out; debriefing was important. But he'd probably take them to a quiet corner of the cafeteria, whereas he intended to take Marina somewhere much more private.

He shepherded her to the staff room; they collected their coats and she grabbed her handbag from her locker. Then he took her back to his flat. During the five-minute walk, she didn't say a word and she was still shivering.

'Where…?' she began as he opened his front door for her and stood aside.

'My flat. I'm making you something to eat,' he said.

'Max, I…'

He smiled wryly. 'Don't worry, I'm not going to leap on you.'

'That wasn't what I was worried about.'

'Then what?'

Her eyes were huge, dark and anguished.

He gave a muffled exclamation and hauled her back into his arms. This time, she wrapped her arms round him too. He kissed the top of her head, feeling as if he were drowning in the scent of rosemary from her hair. He really had to stop this, before it was too late.

But then her arms were round his neck, her fingers were sliding into his hair, and she was pressing tiny kisses into the column of his throat.

It was like lighting touch-paper; the next thing he knew, his mouth was jammed against hers, his arms were wrapped tightly round her and her fingertips were pushing hard against his scalp, urging him on.

Unable to help himself, desperately needing the feel of her bare skin against his fingertips, he untucked her white shirt from the waistband of her tailored, black trousers. He slipped his hands underneath the cotton and splayed his fingers flat against her bare midriff. Her skin felt so soft—and he'd missed this so much.

Then she was doing the same to him, tugging his white shirt out of the waistband of his suit trousers and smoothing her palms along his back.

This was all so familiar, and yet so new at the same time. It was more than four years since

Marina had last touched him like this, and they were different people now, yet they were still the same. They still responded to each other in the same way. It almost felt as though they'd never been apart.

Lost in the moment, Max moved his hands higher, his palms stroking against her ribcage. She inhaled sharply and he traced the lacy edge of her bra with one forefinger. One thing that definitely hadn't changed: Marina still wore ultra-feminine underwear. And right now he really, really wanted to see it. Wanted to see her. Wanted to touch and taste, and let her fill the emptiness inside him.

He undid the buttons of her shirt, his hands shaking; to his relief, she didn't stop him. He pushed the soft cotton off her shoulders, revealing pure-white lace against her slightly olive skin, and desire licked down his spine. He could see her nipples through the lace, hardening as he looked at them, and he just couldn't help himself. He dipped his head, closed his mouth over one nipple through the lace, and sucked hard.

Marina moaned aloud and slid her fingers back

into his hair, urging him on rather than pulling him away, and he was completely lost. He undid the clasp of her bra and let the lace fall to the floor; he cupped her breasts in his hands, remembering their weight and their warmth.

This felt like coming home.

Where he longed to be.

Where he *needed* to be

He wanted Marina so urgently, so desperately. But, more than that, he needed her to want this as much as he did.

He kissed his way up the column of her throat, then took her mouth again, nibbling tiny kisses along her lower lip until she opened her mouth and let him deepen the kiss. Then she was kissing him all the way back, unbuttoning his shirt and tugging it off his shoulders with the same urgency.

Working purely on instinct, Max lifted her up and carried her through to his bedroom, still kissing her. He set her back on her feet again by the window, drew the curtains and switched on the bedside lamp. Still neither of them had said a word; they were lost in a deep, deep hunger and need.

He kissed her again, and then her fingers were

fumbling with the buckle of his belt. Struggling. He gently pushed her hands aside, still kissing her, and dealt with it himself.

He wasn't sure which of them removed which items of clothing, but at last they were how he wanted them to be, skin to skin. And she felt so good: soft and warm, just as he remembered. Just as he dreamed. He drew her closer, and simply fell back on the bed, pulling her with him so she landed on top of him, her glorious hair falling all over his face and her bare skin right next to his.

Heaven.

Marina knew this was all wrong, that she shouldn't be doing this. That Max was off limits. For goodness' sake, he was her ex-husband and her colleague, and when this all blew apart it would be impossible to work together. Not to mention all the mess of their shared past. This was a seriously bad idea.

But she was lying on top of him. Both of them were completely naked, with Max's arms wrapped tightly round her. And, oh, it felt good. Like coming home.

Being in his arms, kissing him, seeing his slate-blue eyes darken almost to black with desire… She'd missed this. Badly. Missed the way Max made her feel as if she were the centre of his universe. Missed the way he made her feel that he were the centre of hers. There was nothing else outside this room, outside this bed. Nothing but the two of them.

The miserable day she'd spent at work, the sense of failure and despair, had all vanished: there was only Max. Max, who was kissing her as if he couldn't get enough of her—just as she couldn't get enough of him.

She shifted slightly, eased a hand between them so she could position the tip of his penis just where she wanted it and gently lowered herself onto him.

Lord, it felt good, the way he filled her, stretched her. The perfect fit. He always had been. Experimentally, she tightened her internal muscles around him.

He sucked in a breath.

And then he began to move. Slowly, at first, then faster, harder, pushing deep inside her. She matched him thrust for thrust, drive for drive, needing this as much as he did. Needing to feel her body sing at his touch. Needing to reaffirm the fact that she was alive, and life was good.

As her climax slammed into her, rippling through her body, Max sat up straight; he wrapped his arms round her and kissed her hard, and she felt the answering pulse of his body.

She had no idea how long they stayed there, locked together, just holding each other, but at last he gently eased out of her. He moved slightly so he could grab the duvet, then pulled it over them both and drew her back into his arms, keeping her close.

Neither of them had said a word since they'd started kissing in his hallway. And Marina was unwilling to break the silence, to shatter this strange peace between them. She simply wrapped her arm round his waist and rested her head against his shoulder.

'Marina,' he said at last. 'I really didn't intend this to happen.'

Was he saying it was a mistake? That he regretted it?

She couldn't bring herself to ask. Couldn't face him rejecting her again.

'I was going to make you something to eat. That was all. Taking you to bed wasn't something I planned.'

'Uh-huh,' she said, carefully keeping her tone noncommittal.

He played with the ends of her hair, just as he had a hundred times before. 'I'm sorry.'

'It's not your fault. I could have said no.' Except she hadn't wanted to. If anything, she'd been the one to incite it. She'd been the one to start the kiss. And she was still here, still naked, still in his bed, still lying in his arms.

'Neither of us was thinking straight.'

She swallowed hard. He could say that again.

He sighed. 'Marina, we need to talk.'

'Not now.' Not when she hadn't got things straight in her head.

'Yes, now,' he insisted. 'There's one elephant in the room we really can't avoid. We both got carried away just now—and neither of us was in a fit state to think about contraception.'

He thought they might have made a baby, an

unplanned child, like they had before? She flinched at the memory. 'There's no need to worry. I'm on the Pill.'

He went very still. 'Are you…seeing someone?'

'It's a bit late to ask now,' she said wryly. 'But I'm not the cheating type; you should know that, Max.'

'I know. Of course you're not.' He grimaced. 'Sorry. I'm not thinking straight.'

Neither was she. 'No, I'm not seeing anyone. As I'm sure Rosie told you.'

'She did,' he admitted. 'So why are you on the Pill? To sort out your periods?'

'Yes. After the…' Her throat closed. Why was it so hard to say that word to him? *Miscarriage*. Ah, hell. He'd know what she meant. One of the biggest elephants in the room. The thing they'd never been able to talk about. The thing that had widened the gap between them day by day, until she hadn't been able to bear it any longer. 'My system went a bit haywire. My GP suggested trying the Pill, and it worked.' She swallowed. 'Though, just in case you were wondering, I don't make a habit of sleeping around. So you won't end up with any—'

He pressed his forefinger lightly against her lips. 'I already know that, and I wouldn't insult you by thinking otherwise. Just for the record,' he added, 'it's the same for me. You're safe.'

'OK. So we know the score.'

'Do we?' He shifted onto his side, so they were looking each other in the face, and gave her a level stare. 'We've spent the last couple of weeks trying to avoid each other as much as possible—and being ultra-polite and professional when we can't.'

She acknowledged the truth of that with a sardonic smile. 'And just now we ripped each other's clothes off and ended up in bed together.'

He gave her a wry smile.

'It's probably because we both needed comfort after the day we've had.'

'Probably,' he agreed.

Oh, that hurt: the acknowledgement that what they'd just shared had simply been comfort for him. Even though she'd been the one to say it, she wished he hadn't agreed with her so quickly.

And then he gave her the most wicked grin. 'So. Mission accomplished?'

'Max Fenton, you're...'

She really hadn't expected that.

How had she possibly forgotten Max's sense of humour—the way he could say something completely inappropriate or surreal and make her laugh? She couldn't help smiling back. 'Yes. Mission accomplished.' She paused. 'You?'

He nodded. 'I think we both needed that.' He stroked her face. 'We always were good together, Marina.'

True. Until it had gone spectacularly wrong.

And then he said something that really shocked her. 'I've missed you.'

She stared at him, not quite believing what she'd just heard. 'What did you say?'

'I've missed you.' His face was utterly open and candid. 'Having you back in my arms just now made me realise how much.'

*He'd missed her.*

And what he'd just said... He could have been speaking for her, too. Given how long they'd been apart, it must have cost him a lot to make that admission. The least she could do was match his honesty. 'I missed you, too,' she said. Making love with him just now—for a while, the empty spaces in her soul had been filled again. Max had made her feel complete, the first time she'd felt that way since they'd separated.

'So where do we go from here?' he asked.

She shook her head. 'I have no idea.'

'Maybe we could start seeing each other?' he suggested.

Was he serious? He really thought that they could pick up where they left off?

'Though we should probably take it slowly,' he added.

She raised an eyebrow. 'Slowly? Considering your bed's all rumpled and I have no idea where my clothes are—or yours…'

He gave her a lopsided grin. 'OK, so we're not very good at doing "slowly".'

She returned the smile. 'We never were. A week, wasn't it?'

'Five and a half days.'

He remembered that precisely—from all those years ago? Marina looked at him, stunned. So was he thinking about the very first time they'd made love? She remembered that night, too. How right it had felt. Even that very first time had been like a kind of homecoming, as if she'd found a place she wanted to be for the rest of her life.

In his arms.

And for four empty years they'd been apart.

'Max, I'm not so sure this is a good idea. I mean, we know that it works between us in bed. But...' She shook her head. 'We crashed and burned last time.'

'I know. But we're both older and wiser now,' Max said, his gaze steady. 'And I think there's still unfinished business between us. Otherwise we wouldn't be right here, right now.'

She swallowed hard. 'We can't change the past.'

'But we can learn from it.'

'And if it all goes wrong again? I don't think I could face picking up the pieces a second time.'

'I don't think either of us is in a fit state to make any sort of decision right now,' he said softly. 'But we do need to talk.'

She blew out a breath. 'About the other elephants in the room? There are quite a few of them.'

'Too many to deal with all at once. But if we tackle them one by one we might stand a chance of sorting it all out.'

'One by one,' she repeated.

'When we're ready. But right now I think you need comfort—because you're one of life's fixers, and you take it personally when you can't make something right. Even if nobody else could've made it right, either.'

Since when had he figured her out that well?

'I need comfort, too,' he said softly. 'Stay with me tonight, Marina.'

'That's your idea of slowly? Asking me to spend the night with you?'

'No. I'm trying to be honest. Right now, I think we both need this.'

'All cats being grey in the dark.' So this was just comfort. Sex. A way of celebrating life when you'd just had to face death.

'Absolutely *not*.' His voice was very clear. 'I wouldn't have done this with anyone else in the department, Marina, and neither would you.'

She couldn't deny the truth of that. She hadn't slept with anyone since Max, even though she'd had offers.

Had he?

It was none of her business what he'd done since she'd walked out. But the idea of Max making love with another woman cut her to the quick. 'I can't stay. I can't go to work tomorrow in these clothes.'

'I have a washer-dryer. I can put your stuff through the machine overnight, and your clothes will be clean for the morning. And I have a spare toothbrush.'

It was an easy solution. And she was oh, so tempted. She normally wore dark trousers and a white or cream shirt at work, so it wasn't as if it would be obvious that she was wearing the same clothes. She could stay, spend the rest of the evening in bed with Max, exorcising some of their demons. Comforting each other.

*Making love.* Because it wouldn't be just sex— not for her.

'The sensible thing,' she said, while she still had a few vestiges of self-control, 'Would be for me to go home.'

He cupped her face with one hand, tracing her lower lip with the pad of his thumb. 'We've had a rough day; it's not the time for being sensible. You need to be held and so do I.'

'But you've seen worse than today if you've been working for Doctors Without Borders.'

He frowned. 'How do you know about that?'

'Rosie told me.' She paused. 'Why did you go?'

'I thought we weren't talking about any of the elephants. Besides, I promised to feed you.'

'Why did you go?' she repeated.

He shrugged and sat up, drawing his knees up to his chest and wrapping his arms round them. 'If you really want to know, it felt like the right thing to do. You'd gone to London, and I didn't want to stay in Bristol without you. There were too many memories and I was miserable. I hated going home to that empty flat. To me it showed I was a failure, that I couldn't make my marriage work.'

She couldn't let him take complete responsibility for the break-up. That wasn't fair. 'It wasn't just your fault, Max. There were two of us in that marriage, and I was the one who left.'

He reached out to touch her cheek for a moment. 'Thank you for that. But I still felt a failure, and facing it every day was too much for me. I couldn't fix my own problems, but working for Doctors Without Borders meant I could make a difference to other people's lives. And I really needed to feel that I could do that. That I could fix *something*.'

She could understand that. Wasn't that part of the reason why she worked in emergency medicine, so she could make a difference?

He looked down at her, unsmiling. 'As we're tackling elephants, why did you—' He stopped abruptly. 'Why did you leave Bristol?'

She knew exactly what he'd been going to ask: why had she walked out on him? Because he'd shut her out and she'd felt that she was the only one making an effort in their marriage. 'Same reason as you,' she said. 'I was miserable in Bristol. Every time I walked through the city centre I saw pregnant women, and I couldn't handle it.' Maybe this was going too far, but she was going to be honest with him. She dragged in a breath. 'I needed support, Max.' Support that Max and his family wouldn't—or couldn't?—give her. 'You shut me out. And what happened to us… It was more than I could deal with on my own. I needed you and you just weren't there. So I came home, because I knew my family would help me get through it. I knew at least here that I'd be loved.'

He still wasn't smiling, and his expression was unreadable. 'Enough elephants for now, I think. Though I do owe you an apology.' He swallowed hard. 'For not giving you what you needed.'

And in that moment Marina realised. The way he'd acted back then wasn't because he hadn't cared. It was because he hadn't known how to deal with the situation, either. 'I was the one who walked out.' She hadn't stayed to fight for him. 'So I guess we're even. I owe you an apology, too.'

He spread his hands, the gesture telling her he didn't know what to say.

That made two of them.

And the breakup of their marriage was too complicated for them to work out in a single conversation.

'I'll make us something to eat.' He paused. 'So, do you want me to put your stuff in the washing machine?'

Working for Doctors Without Borders had clearly made him more practical. The old Max wouldn't even have thought about it until the next morning—when it would've been much too late to do anything about it.

*Stay or go?*

If she stayed, she knew she'd end up making love with him again. Clouding the issues between them.

But, if she left, he'd take it as a rejection and he'd clam up on her. Which meant they would never get the closure they both needed. They'd still be stuck in limbo, unable to move on.

Sleeping with Max didn't mean that she was still in love with him, or that he was in love with her. They'd already agreed that for tonight this was just comfort—comfort of a kind that only they could give each other. No strings.

Should she stay or should she go?

# CHAPTER SIX

'ONE thing: this is just tonight? No strings?'
Marina asked.

Max's expression was completely unreadable.
'No strings.'

'Then, yes. I'll stay.'

'OK.' He climbed out of bed, grabbed a pair
of jeans from his wardrobe, pulled them on, then
took a navy bathrobe from the back of the door
and handed it to her. 'If you want a shower
before you come downstairs, the bathroom's first
on the left—and the towels are clean.'

'Thanks.'

Considering how well they knew each other's
bodies, and what they'd just done, Marina knew
it was ridiculous to wait until he'd left the room
before climbing out of bed. But she did so
anyway, feeling shy—as well as enormously

grateful that Max had clearly picked up on it and wasn't putting any pressure on her.

Max's bathroom turned out to be very plain and functional, just like his bedroom. Then again, he hadn't been in London for long. Less than a month. Given that Max had been working abroad, his things were probably still in storage. Certainly she'd seen nothing she remembered from their old flat in Bristol. When she'd left Max, she'd taken only her clothes, a few books, precious photographs and her omelette pan, not wanting anything around to remind her of the disaster of their marriage.

Another off-limits topic, unless they wanted to tackle another elephant. Though right at that moment Marina thought it would be better to keep things light. Extremely light. Especially as they'd agreed that tonight meant no strings.

She stepped out of the shower, dried herself then pulled his bathrobe on and drew the belt tight. The robe was soft to the touch and smelled of him; it felt like being wrapped in his arms.

She padded through to the kitchen. Max had obviously collected her clothes on the way; she could hear the gentle whirring of the washing machine, and he'd put the kettle on to make coffee.

Though she couldn't see any sign of the food he'd promised.

'OK?' he asked.

She nodded. 'And hungry. Do you want a hand?'

'Thanks.' He smiled wryly. 'You know, I really was going to be nice and make you dinner.'

'But?' Something in his expression made her brave. Cheeky. She opened the first cupboard, peered inside and raised an eyebrow when she saw it was completely empty. And so was the next one. 'I see. You did some training at Old Mother Hubbard's school of cookery.'

He rolled his eyes. 'Very funny. Not everyone likes cooking, you know.'

Didn't they? 'You used to enjoy it.'

'No, I used to like being in a kitchen with you,' he corrected. 'You used to do the actual cooking. I just fetched things and washed up and talked to you.'

She hadn't thought of it that way. She just remembered doing what she always did with her family, everyone joining in and doing a bit, talking, laughing and singing as they washed up, mixed, tasted and cooked—the normal things that families did together. She remembered preparing meals with Max, sharing a single glass of wine with him, and half the time having a long break between preparing the meal and actually cooking it, because they'd ended up in bed together, needing to sate desire more than they'd needed to sate hunger.

She looked in his fridge. There was a lump of cheese he hadn't wrapped up properly that was going hard round the edges, a carton of orange juice and a carton of milk. So he didn't even have the makings of an omelette or a basic dish of pasta with tomato sauce. And he didn't have a fruit bowl of any description. 'Max, this is atrocious. No wonder you're so thin. Do you eat at all?'

'Of course I do.'

'Like what? Do you live on takeaway food or something?'

'Anyone would think you were the food police,' he grumbled. 'There's nothing wrong with takeaways.'

'In moderation. But it's not the same as eating a properly balanced meal.'

'All right, if you must know, I normally eat at the hospital canteen at lunchtime so I don't need to do more than make myself a sandwich when I get in.'

She couldn't help laughing. 'A fresh-air sandwich, would that be? And an invisible piece of fruit?'

He sighed. 'I admit, I'm out of bread right now. And fruit. I forgot to buy some today.'

'Uh-huh.' That wasn't all he'd forgotten to buy, from the look of it.

He rolled his eyes. 'Don't rub it in. So I'm out of sandwich fillings as well.'

'I noticed.'

'And I'm *not* too thin.'

'No?' She raised an eyebrow. 'My mother would take one look at you, make you sit down at the kitchen table and start cooking for you. I bet Rosie said something to you too, didn't she?'

'Well—yes,' he admitted. 'But your family doesn't do subtle.'

'No.' Though he'd never seemed to mind. She was used to people being open and honest rather than reserved and masking their true feelings with a polite smile. It was so much easier to sort out any problems if you talked about them, instead of expecting the other person to guess what was going on inside your head, the way Max's family seemed to do.

'That wasn't a criticism, by the way,' Max added.

'Wasn't it?'

'No. I've always liked your family. Even when they're being really full on.'

Because her family always acted out of love, Marina thought. There were no hidden agendas. You always knew exactly where they were coming from, and they said exactly what they meant.

He pulled open a kitchen drawer and extracted a handful of leaflets. 'Since we've established that neither of us is going to be cooking tonight, and I promised to feed you, I'll order a takeaway. What would you like?'

'I don't mind, as long as there isn't a really long wait.' Her stomach rumbled, as if to make the point, and she grimaced. 'Sorry.'

'It's OK. Neither of us had time for lunch today. I'm hungry too,' he said.

'If you have a corner shop nearby that sells eggs, I could make us an omelette,' she offered. 'That'd be quicker than a takeaway.'

'Technical hitch,' Max said. 'I don't actually have an omelette pan.'

Because she'd taken it with her when she'd left. Somehow it didn't surprise her that he hadn't replaced it. 'Do you have any saucepans of any description?'

'My kitchen isn't that bad.'

By her standards, it was. 'Yes or no, Max?'

He opened a cupboard door to show her. 'Satisfied?'

'I can work with them, sure. If you can go and buy some eggs, bacon, cream, dried pasta and salad,' she said, 'I'll make us pasta carbonara. It'll take ten minutes.'

'So much for me looking after you,' Max said wryly.

'As you just said, not everyone likes cooking. You don't—but I do. It soothes me,' she said. 'And, if I'd been thinking straight, I would've suggested going back to mine.'

'Would you?' Max asked, giving her a searching look.

She wrinkled her nose. 'Truthfully? No. I wouldn't have asked you into my space. But there's no way I'm going back to my flat right now wearing nothing but your bathrobe. So if you want feeding you'll have to go to the shop. What did I do with my handbag?'

'Uh—I put it over here.' Clearly he'd retrieved it, along with her clothes, from wherever she'd dropped it. 'But this was my suggestion, so I'm paying. I'll be back in a tick.' He pulled on a sweater and a pair of battered running shoes and left.

While Max was gone, Marina laid the table in the kitchen, rummaged in his almost-bare cupboards to find the equipment she needed then wandered into his living room. It was as spartan as his kitchen and bedroom; there were no pictures on the walls, no photographs anywhere, and nothing personal to give a single clue about the person who lived in the flat. There were a few medical textbooks on the bookshelves, but that was all. The décor and furnishings were completely neutral, and his sofa didn't have so much as a cushion to soften its stark lines.

Max's flat wasn't a home, it was just a place to sleep. He might just as well be living out of a suitcase, and it made her heart ache for him. How different it was from her own flat, filled with colour, photographs and memories.

She shook herself. It was none of her business any more. He'd signed the papers. They were officially divorced.

Yet here she was, cutting the hard edges off the lonely lump of cheese in his fridge and grating the rest of it into a small bowl.

She must be mad.

She'd been here before, had her heart broken into tiny pieces that had taken years to glue back together. Yet Max's words kept echoing in her head.

*We're both older and wiser now.*

*And I think there's still unfinished business between us.*

Was he right? Could they learn from the past, try again and avoid the mistakes?

Somewhere deep inside, she felt a flicker of something that might just have been hope.

\* \* \*

When Max came back from the corner shop and walked into the kitchen, it didn't feel anything like the room he was used to in his rented flat. He couldn't quite put his finger on what the shift was: simply that Marina had laid the table for two and was sitting there, mug of coffee in hand, flicking through a medical journal.

'Sorry—I took liberties with your kettle and your magazine,' she said. 'Hope you don't mind.'

'Of course not.' He handed her the carrier bag. 'Is this lot all OK?' He'd remembered the brief shopping list she'd given him—eggs, bacon, cream, salad and dried pasta—and added a loaf of bread, plus a decent bottle of Pinot Grigio he'd found in the chiller cabinet.

She looked through them, then glanced up at him and smiled. 'Fabulous. Do you want to sort the salad while I do this?'

'Sure.'

'Did you want a coffee? The kettle's still hot.'

'No, I'm fine. But thanks for asking.'

It felt oddly domestic, washing the salad and placing it in a bowl; Max was surprised to discover how much he'd missed being in a kitchen with her. He enjoyed watching Marina cook, the deft way she beat the eggs with the cream, then kept an eye on the pasta at the same time as she was dry-frying the bacon. For the very first time since he'd moved into the flat, the kitchen smelled fantastic. It reminded him of the way it had been when they'd first moved in together, how he'd teased her that she could go on one of those TV shows where people were given random ingredients, and however strange they were that she would manage to come up with something edible—a feast, even.

Although he remembered Marina avidly flicking through foodie magazines, she hardly ever stuck to a recipe; she used them as spring-boards for her own imagination. And most of the time she cooked without weighing things, either—a practice he guessed was born from cooking with her mother and her sister from an early age.

As he opened the wine and poured two glasses, she dished up—Max noticed that she'd warmed the plates, too, which he would never have bothered doing—and they sat opposite each other at his kitchen table. Familiar, comfortable, just like he'd done so many times before. He was glad then that he'd agreed to her request of no strings; it avoided any awkwardness between them. Because he wouldn't have missed sharing this with her, not for the world.

If somehow they could pick their way through the mess of the past, work out how to make a new start…

Too far, too fast. There was a long way to go before they could start to do that.

But it was years since he'd felt that weird lightness inside, a feeling that took him a while to pin down and categorise as hope.

He took a mouthful of the pasta. 'This is fantastic.'

'It's the best comfort food I know,' she said. Then she gave him a speaking look. 'It's not exactly *difficult* to make, Max. And it's practically as quick as making a sandwich.'

He forbore to comment, knowing that he'd never bother to cook for himself; it didn't seem worth it, cooking for one. But he loved the fact that she'd made it for him and didn't fish for extravagant compliments on her skills. She was secure in who she was, and didn't need anyone to pump her ego for her. He'd always liked that about Marina, her self-sufficiency.

And then, when she'd crumbled, he hadn't known what to do. What to say. How to make things right. He'd panicked and buried himself in work to block out the feeling of failure. Except the sense of failure had only deepened when he realised that he'd pushed her away, that she'd walked out on him.

'The wine's lovely,' she said.

'I'm glad you like it. You always used to prefer white wine to red, as long as it wasn't oaky.'

She blinked. 'You remembered that?'

'Yes.' There were a lot of other things he remembered about her: the shape of her body fitting against his as he fell asleep; the scent of her hair—and the shadows in her eyes. The shadows they weren't going to talk about tonight, but that he knew were still there—just masked for a little while until they worked out how to deal with them.

After dinner, they washed up together. Although they didn't say much, it was a companionable silence rather than the loaded silence that had haunted the end of their marriage. Max switched the washing machine over to the tumble-drying cycle, then ushered her through into the living room. 'Sorry, I haven't got round to sorting out a television. Though, if you really want to, we could maybe watch a film on my laptop.'

She smiled. 'You're trying too hard, Max. I'm fine. Though, if you want to put some music on, that'd be nice.'

'Music I can do.' He connected his MP3 player to the small speakers, selected a playlist of the mellow kind of music he remembered she used to like, and topped up their glasses before joining her on the sofa. He rested the arm nearest to her along the back of the sofa, and was relieved when she curled into him, letting him curve his arm along her shoulders.

'When did you move in here?' she asked.

'The day before I started working at the hospital.'

'So most of your stuff is still in storage?'

He shrugged. 'I travel light nowadays. I guess it's

a hangover from working with Doctors Without Borders; I got used to living out of a suitcase.'

'What made you come back to England?'

'Do you really want to talk about another elephant?' he asked softly.

She was silent, but he waited, guessing that she was thinking about it.

'No,' she said finally. 'We said no strings tonight. That means no elephants.'

'Well, that's your answer.' He didn't want to tell her about the accident, because he didn't want her to pity him. And he didn't want to tell her about his father, because it would be all too easy to tell her the whole story—and he still hadn't quite come to terms with it himself. 'We're going to have to talk about it properly at some point. But you're right: not now.'

'We've made a start,' Marina said. 'That's enough for tonight.'

They lapsed back into silence, but it was still a comfortable silence, and she was still cuddling into him. Right at that moment he was happy just to be there with her in his arms, chilling out and forgetting about their lousy day.

When the music finally ended, he said, 'I think we could both do with some sleep. Come to bed.' He stood up and held his hand out; when she took it, he pulled her to her feet, twined his fingers through hers and led her back to his bedroom.

She bit her lip, looking faintly embarrassed.

'What?'

'Max, I'm not wearing anything under this robe.'

Guessing what was making her uncomfortable, he lifted her hand to his mouth, kissed her palm and curled her fingers round where he'd kissed. 'I know that. OK. Turn your back.'

'Why?'

'So I can get undressed too.' He gave her a wicked grin. 'Unless you'd rather watch me take all my clothes off? I can strip for you, if you like.'

Colour shot into her face. 'Max!'

'Just a thought,' he said mildly. But at least he'd made her smile.

He pulled off his sweater, and stifled a chuckle when she hastily turned her back to him. He stripped swiftly, climbed into the bed and pulled the duvet over him. 'OK, I'm in bed—and my back's turned, so it's safe for you to take off my robe and get into bed.'

He felt the mattress dip slightly with her weight, then she curled into him. 'Thank you.' She pressed a kiss against his spine.

'What for?'

'Being nice. When I'm behaving ridiculously, in the circumstances.'

He shifted so that he was facing her. 'It's not a problem.' He kissed the tip of her nose. 'Good night, Marina.'

'Good night.'

He turned the light off. It was a while before he slept, though he was aware when she fell asleep, as her breathing became regular and deep. With Marina lying in his arms, he felt oddly at peace. Funny, in his brief relationships over the last couple of years, he'd never once stayed the night with anyone. He realised now how much he'd missed that closeness.

Ha. Who was he trying to kid? More like, how much he'd missed Marina. And that was why he'd never spent the night with anyone else. Because they hadn't been her.

Finally, Max slid into sleep.

* * *

'No!'

The agonised yell woke Marina instantly. She sat bolt upright, slightly disoriented and wondering where she was.

Then it all snapped back. She was in Max's flat. Max's bed. And Max was thrashing about next to her, clearly in the middle of a nightmare. His breathing was fast and shallow; he was almost at the point of hyperventilating.

She laid a hand on his shoulder and shook him. 'Max. *Max*. It's OK. You're here. In London. With me.'

He groaned and shuddered; she continued talking to him, reassuring him quietly, until at last he was still.

'Max?' she asked softly. 'Are you OK?'

'Uh, fine.'

She didn't believe him. 'You were having a nightmare.'

'I'm fine. Sorry for waking you.' He sounded embarrassed.

'It's not a problem.' She sighed. 'If I knew where your bedside light was, I'd turn it on.'

Without comment, he switched on the lamp.

His face looked absolutely ghastly, very pale, and he was in a cold sweat. Whatever he'd been dreaming about, it had clearly been distressing in the extreme. 'Stay put,' she said. 'I'll get you some water.' She retrieved the bathrobe, belted it tightly round herself, then fetched him a glass of water and sat on the bed next to him.

He took a sip of water and placed the glass on his bedside table.

'So what was that about?' she asked.

'Nothing.'

She laced her fingers through his and simply waited.

Eventually, he sighed. 'I get bad dreams from time to time.'

'About something that happened while you were working abroad?' she asked.

'Yes.'

'Tell me.'

He shook his head. 'It's old stuff.'

She had no idea where he'd been working—whether it had been a war zone, or whether he'd been helping out after some kind of natural disaster—so she couldn't even begin to imagine what he'd seen to affect him so badly. 'Did you have any counselling about it?'

'I didn't need it.'

'Tell me,' she said neutrally. 'If a colleague had been through whatever it was you went through, would you advise them to have counselling?'

'I'm fine. Don't fuss.'

She'd seen that look on his face before—when he'd shut himself away from her, after she'd miscarried their baby. Clearly this was one respect in which he hadn't changed. Even now, Max was pushing her away, refusing to talk.

Maybe she should take the hint.

'I think,' she said quietly, releasing his hand, 'maybe I should go home.'

He glanced at the clock. 'It's three in the morning. The Tube won't be open.'

'I'll call a taxi, then.'

'Marina.' He sat upright and wrapped his arms round her. 'I'm sorry. Don't go. It's...not that easy for me to talk about things.'

She wasn't going to throw his apology back in his face; four years ago she might've done that, but as he'd said himself she was older and wiser now. Instead, she slid her arms round him, and he rested his forehead on her shoulder.

'I was working as part of the rescue team after an earthquake. While I was stabilising a little girl so we'd be able to move her, there was a second tremor—and the building came down on us. It took them a while to dig us out.'

'How long?'

'I was unconscious for some of it.'

'How long?' she repeated.

'I don't know. Five or six hours, maybe. It was pretty unpleasant. Hot as hell; my mouth and eyes and nose were full of dust, and I couldn't even move to clean it out.'

She tightened her arms round him. She'd just bet that it had been far worse than his economical description. And he'd been unconscious. 'Did you have concussion?'

'Yes.'

'And?'

He sighed. 'A broken arm and leg. Which meant I wasn't much use out there, so they shipped me home.'

And no doubt he'd been stuck in bed for a while. No wonder he understood exactly what Rosie was going through.

Though Marina was very, very aware of what he *hadn't* said. And she knew he wasn't going to volunteer the information himself. 'What about the little girl?' she asked quietly.

'She didn't make it.'

Four little words that told her volumes. 'And losing that patient today must've brought some of the memories back,' she said.

'Yes.' He closed his eyes. 'I suppose I really should've warned you that I might dream about it tonight. But we—uh—I thought I'd be OK.'

Except he wasn't. 'Then I'm glad I stayed,' she said, stroking his face. 'That I could be here for you.'

'I'm glad you stayed, too,' he admitted.

Then somehow his mouth was on hers, warm and sweet, asking rather than demanding, yet giving and promising at the same time.

This time, their love-making was slow and gentle, soothing each other rather than filling them with the frantic and desperate need from before. Every touch, every kiss, was like balm being poured over old hurts. This time, Marina's climax was soft, sweet and fulfilling, like summer rain rather than a winter cloudburst. And when Max turned out the light she curled back into his arms and drifted into sleep, feeling warm, safe and secure—and happier than she'd felt in a long, long time.

# CHAPTER SEVEN

THE alarm shrilled; Marina rolled over and groped for the bedside table, intending to hit the snooze button, then suddenly realised why the bedside table wasn't there: because she wasn't in her own bed. And Max's alarm clock was over on his side.

She heard a soft click, and the shrilling stopped.

'Good morning,' Max said, his tone completely neutral.

She followed his lead. 'Good morning.'

And now what? She'd never experienced morning-after awkwardness before—not even the first time she'd spent the night with Max. They'd gone to bed laughing, and they'd woken up tangled together and smiling.

Now they were tangled together and...awkward.

'What's the time?' she asked.

'Half-past six.'

An hour and a half until her shift started. And she had things to do. She really, really shouldn't be here. 'Then I have to go. I need to collect Phoebe from Neil, and I need to take her to see Rosie before she goes to the hospital nursery.'

'I'll sort your clothes out while you have a shower, if you like?' Max offered.

'Thanks. That'd be good.'

By the time she'd finished, Max had laid her clothes on the bed—he'd clearly taken them straight out of the dryer rather than ironing them, as they were a little crumpled, but nobody would notice beneath her coat—and she could smell coffee and toast. She went into the kitchen, and Max handed her a mug. 'I've added a bit of cold water so you can drink it straight down.' He also handed her a plate of buttered toast. 'Sorry, I don't have any jam or honey.'

That wry, slightly shy smile, made her decide: Max, too, clearly felt awkward and mixed up about the whole situation, not sure whether he was more relieved or disappointed that she was leaving.

'No jam or honey. Now, why doesn't that surprise me, Dr Hubbard?' she teased.

'Yeah, yeah.' But his face cleared.

She walked over to him and kissed him lightly. 'Thanks, Max. I appreciate this.'

'Is there anything else you need?'

'I'm fine—but thank you for asking.' She finished her toast and drank her coffee quickly. 'In case you were wondering, I really do have to go. It's not just an excuse to avoid you.' Well, not completely. Though she had to admit that it was pretty convenient.

'Uh-huh. I'll see you at work.'

She bit her lip. 'Max, before I go…'

He looked at her. 'What?'

'About last night… I don't want anyone talking about us at work. Can we keep this to ourselves?'

'Sure.' His face was expressionless. 'As you said, no strings.'

She saw the flicker of hurt in his eyes before he managed to mask it. And, even though she knew this was going to lead to complications and was completely dangerous where her peace of mind was concerned, she said, 'I'm not on call tonight, so you could come over for supper, if you like?'

He looked at her for a moment, as if judging whether her offer was genuine or guilt-driven.

It was a bit of both, if she were honest about it.

'I'd like that,' he said finally. 'What time?'

'Seven? That gives me time to take Phoebe to Rosie after my shift and stay with them for a bit.'

'Are you sure that's long enough? I can make it half-past seven, if that's easier.'

'Half-past seven it is. Got a piece of paper and a pen?'

'Sure.' He grabbed a pad and pen from the drawer where he kept the takeaway leaflets and handed it to her.

She scribbled down her address, added a mobile-phone number, then kissed him briefly. 'See you later. I have to run.'

The world seemed a different place this morning, Max thought as he showered. He hadn't felt this relaxed and carefree for years—now he thought about it, not since he and Marina had first been together. There wasn't the worry that had come with her pregnancy and the hurried arrangements for their wedding, or the desolation that had surrounded her miscarriage, or the misery as their marriage had splintered, or the days afterwards when he'd worked to the point of near-exhaustion so that he'd be able to fall into a dreamless sleep and shut out the past.

Then he realised why he felt so relaxed.

Because, for the first time in a long, long while, there was hope in his life.

He knew that he and Marina still had a long way to go; for a start, they had to tackle the things that had gone so badly wrong before, and work through them together instead of running away from the issues. But he was beginning to think that maybe now there was a chance that they could come out the other side. That he could make it with her.

He smiled at everyone on his way in to work that morning, but, even though his heart gave a funny little jolt when he saw Marina, he was careful to treat her the way he usually did, as if she were just another member of the team.

And everything, Max thought, was definitely all right with his world today.

'Someone, please, help my baby!'

The woman staggering into reception was carrying a child Marina judged to be around five years old; her face was white with fear, and the child was wheezing. An asthma attack? Marina wondered.

'Can you tell Max I need him in Resus, please?' she said to Dawn, the staff nurse who was doing triage.

Dawn nodded and went to find Max as Marina walked over to the woman. 'I'm a doctor. Let me help you,' she said, taking the child. 'We'll go into a room over here. Can you tell me what happened?'

'Jessie's had an ear infection; the doctor gave her antibiotics and she was perking up. I took her to the park because I thought some fresh air might make her feel better, but then she started wheezing. She can't breathe!'

A first glance also told Marina that the child was covered in a rash, tiny red spots that she could practically see appearing on the little girl's skin.

'I know I should've called an ambulance, but the park's opposite the hospital and I thought it would be quicker to bring her over.'

'You did the right thing,' Marina reassured her. 'What were the antibiotics?'

'Amoxicillin.'

'Has your daughter ever had amoxicillin before?'

'No.'

'When did you start giving it to her?'

'Last week. She had the last dose last night. The doctor said it was important to finish them, even if she seemed a lot better.'

To help avoid antibiotic resistance—funnily enough, the topic that Marina had planned to cover in her next batch of articles. 'How long has she had the rash?'

'She had a couple of spots this morning, but...' The woman gasped as she saw the redness over the little girl's face. 'It wasn't anywhere near that bad. I would never have taken her out with that!'

They could practically see the spots appearing and spreading. 'I think,' Marina said carefully, 'Your daughter's reacting to the antibiotics.'

'But—I thought if they were allergic to antibiotics it happened straight away?'

'Sometimes it does, but it often happens a day or so after the last dose,' Marina explained. 'You did the right thing bringing her here, because we can help her. Is she on any other medication?'

'No.'

'Does she have any other medical conditions or allergies?'

The woman shook her head. 'Just the normal coughs and colds kids get, and she was definitely over the ear infection, because she'd stopped saying how much it hurts.'

Marina established the rest of Jessie's patient history on the way to Resus. As they reached the double doors, Max came up. 'This is Max Fenton, our senior registrar,' Marina said. 'Max, this is Jessie, and I think she's having a reaction to amoxicillin.'

'OK.' Max smiled at Jessie's mother. 'I know you're worried, but your daughter's in the best place now. Dawn here will take you through to the relatives' room, and we'll come and get you when Jessie's feeling a bit better.'

The woman shook her head wildly. 'I can't leave my baby. I *can't*.'

'The thing is,' Marina said, 'the medical procedures we need to use can look a bit scary, and we might not have time to explain them to you properly as we're working. I know waiting's going to be hard, but trust me on this. It'll be a lot easier on your nerves than watching us.'

Jessie's mother looked at her. 'You're the doctor in the paper, aren't you?'

'Yes.' Marina gave her a self-conscious smile.

'I read your column every week. It's really good.' She nodded. 'All right.'

While Dawn took the woman through to the relatives' room, Marina filled Max in on Jessie's medical history.

Gently, they removed Jessie's coat and sweater; the rash had spread, and the little girl was fighting for air.

'We'll defer intubation until the epinephrine kicks in,' Max said.

'I'll give her high-flow oxygen and salbutamol on mask,' Marina said.

'Good.' Max deftly put a line into Jessie's vein as Marina hooked her up to the monitoring equipment.

'BP's low,' Marina said. With severe allergic reactions, blood could leak from the veins, causing low blood pressure and hypovolaemic shock.

'Give her a bolus of Ringer's,' Max said. 'How old is she?'

'Five.'

'Normal weight—I'd say about eighteen kilos.'

'Agreed.' Marina mentally calculated the amount of solution she needed to give, based on the child's weight, and sorted it out while Max put in a second line and administered epinephrine.

It took three doses before Jessie finally stopped fighting for air; Max added antihistamines to the mix, and Marina kept a close eye on the monitoring equipment, knowing that the drugs they were using to stabilise the little girl's condition and stop the swelling of her throat could also cause heart arrhythmias.

'I'll call the paediatric ward and tell them we want to admit Jessie,' Marina said. 'We need her under obs for the next twenty-four hours.' With severe drug reactions, there was a risk of a second, delayed reaction, so it was best to be prepared. 'And that rash is going to be incredibly itchy—she'll need some cream as well as the antihistamines.'

By the time Marina had called up to the children's ward and spoken to Lynne, the senior sister on the ward, Jessie had revived sufficiently to want her mother. Max was holding the little girl's hand and telling her a story to distract her, and he was making a great job of it; anyone would think he had children of his own and was used to telling stories at the drop of a hat to ward off tears.

Marina pushed away the thought of what might have been and said, 'I'll go and get her mum.'

The little girl brightened as soon as she saw her mother, and the woman almost collapsed in relief when she saw that her child was safe, and hugged her tightly.

'She's very much on the mend now,' Marina said. 'But we're going to keep her in overnight. When a child reacts to medication as severely as Jessie did, sometimes there's a second reaction a few hours later, so we want to make sure she's OK before she goes home.'

'The rash will take a bit longer to go. It'll probably last for about a week,' Max said. 'And it'll look worse before it gets better—it often seems to work its way downwards. We can give Jessie some antihistamines to make sure she doesn't swell up and to help with the rash.'

'But it'll be terribly itchy, worse even than chickenpox,' Marina added. 'So we'll give you some lotion to help with that. Lynne on the children's ward is brilliant with kids, and she'll show you ways of helping Jessie to press or pinch her skin rather than scratch. I'll take you up and introduce you to the team—Rhys Morgan, the consultant there, is just *lovely.*'

There was a particular softness to Marina's smile as she said the other man's name, and Max had to suppress a sudden flare of jealousy. How ridiculous. Despite what had happened last night, he had no claims on Marina—though she'd told him that she wasn't seeing anyone. He didn't have the right to be jealous.

Or maybe last night really had been all about comfort, and although she wasn't actually seeing the paediatric specialist she was attracted to him. In love with him, even.

He pushed the thought away. 'We'll tell your GP what's happened and make sure that Jessie's hospital records are labelled, so the medical teams all know to give her a different sort of antibiotic rather than penicillin if she needs treatment in the future,' he said to Jessie's mother. 'Though it's worth getting one of those Medic-Alert bracelets in case you're elsewhere in the country or if you go abroad—it'll warn the medics that she's allergic to penicillin-type antibiotics.'

'I will. Thank you both so much. You've been brilliant.'

'It's what we're here for.' Marina smiled at her. 'Come on, I'll take you both up so Jessie can get settled in to the ward.'

Max watched her leave before he started on the

paperwork. They were definitely good together at work—and he hoped they could sort things out so they were good together outside work, too. The way it used to be, before everything had gone wrong.

# CHAPTER EIGHT

AT EXACTLY half-past seven that evening, Max rang Marina's doorbell. Her flat was a twenty-minute walk in the opposite direction to his from the hospital, though it was a pleasant walk, past two parks and in a road lined with trees.

A few moments later, she answered the door. Tonight she was dressed in a black, crinkle-pleated, silky skirt that fell almost to her ankles, a matching vest-top and a bright-pink georgette shirt which she'd used as an unstructured jacket; her hair was down, and her feet were bare apart from the nail polish on her toes that matched her shirt. She looked incredibly feminine and Max found it difficult to resist the urge to yank her into his arms and kiss her until both their heads were spinning—but the sensible side of him reminded him that it was a bad idea to push her too hard or too fast. He wanted her to relax with him. So he simply smiled and handed her a bunch of deep-blue irises. 'For you.'

'Thank you, Max.' She looked stunned, then pleased.

Did she really think he'd forget her favourite flowers that quickly?

'I wasn't sure what you were cooking, so I thought I'd play it safe.' He gave her the bottle of chilled Sauvignon Blanc.

'That's lovely. Though you really didn't need to bring anything—it's only supper.'

'I wanted to,' he said simply. 'And I didn't want you to think that I'm taking you for granted.'

'Come in. I'll put these in some water.'

He followed her into the flat.

There were photographs hanging in the narrow hallway, and he'd just bet the mantelpiece in her living room was crammed with more framed photographs. There was a cork board in her kitchen with photographs and postcards pinned to it; some of the photos were clearly of work nights out, as he recognised several of their colleagues, and others were of Marina's family.

Several sheets of artwork were fastened to the fridge with magnets—abstract patterns of thick paint, liberally sprinkled with glitter, which he guessed were Phoebe's. Pots of herbs grew on the windowsill, and there was a spice rack on the worktop that Max knew from experience was well used rather than just sitting there for decorative effect.

Marina's kitchen was obviously the heart of her flat, just as it had been in their home together; and suddenly he felt wistful. He could remember how it had felt to come home on days when their duties hadn't matched; walking into a room had been like walking into her arms for a hug, even when she wasn't there, because everywhere had felt so welcoming.

So different from his almost-empty flat.

And so very different from his parents' ultra-formal house, where he felt guilty about putting a dent into a pristine cushion and wouldn't dream of putting his feet up on the sofa.

In Marina's flat, he instantly felt at home. It made him realise again how much he'd missed her. How empty his life had been since he'd lost her.

Could they give each other a second chance?

'Sorry, I'm running a teensy bit behind, so dinner's going to be another twenty minutes. Do you want a coffee, or do you want to start on the wine?' she asked.

'Coffee would be lovely,' he said politely.

She put the wine in the fridge and switched on the kettle. 'Make yourself comfortable. You can go through into the living room, if you like, and I'll bring our coffee through.'

'Do you mind if I sit here?' He indicated one of the chairs at her kitchen table.

'Sure. Help yourself.' She smiled at him and started arranging the irises in a clear-glass vase.

'Anything I can do to help?'

'You can get the milk out of the fridge, if you like.' She busied herself shaking coffee grounds into a cafetière.

He opened the fridge and blinked. 'Your fridge is full,' he said as he retrieved the milk and set it on the worktop.

'That's what a normal person's fridge looks like.' She laughed. 'Yours *isn't* normal, Dr Hubbard.'

The only answer he could give to that was a

wry smile, and a change of subject. 'Something smells wonderful.'

'Supper,' she said, frothing the milk in a jug with a tiny whisk before adding it to the coffee and handing him a mug.

It was typical of Marina to make proper coffee rather than instant, he thought, and to add those extra touches without making a big deal out of it.

'Sorry, I haven't had time to lay the table yet.'

'I'll do it, if you tell me where everything is,' Max offered.

'Sure. Cutlery's in the second drawer along, place-mats are in the drawer next to them, and the glasses are on the middle shelf of the cupboard above the kettle.'

So she still kept everything in the same places as she'd kept things in their kitchen. No wonder he felt as if he knew his way around already.

'I didn't get a chance to see Rosie today,' he said. 'How's she doing?'

'OK, but horribly bored,' Marina replied. 'Mind you, I don't think I'd cope too well with being confined to a hospital bed.'

Max certainly hadn't. He'd brooded and brooded and brooded. Then again, he'd had a lot to brood about. Finding a new job, dealing with his father's death—and then coming to terms with the bombshell his father had left. Not to mention the sea-change in his own feelings afterwards, losing his respect for his father and discovering a new sympathy towards his mother, even at the same time as he loathed the way she fussed over him and smothered him. 'Spending a day in bed with a book is a treat. But if you're forced to do it for a month it'll drive you crazy.'

She raised an eyebrow. 'That sounded personal, Max. Is that what happened to you after the earthquake?'

He backtracked swiftly. Marina didn't know any of the stuff about his family, and he wasn't going to burden her with it, despite the fact that she'd asked. 'Yes. And I know other people who've been stuck on bed rest. Not for pre-eclampsia, admittedly, but the principle's the same.'

'So that's why you visit her almost every day?'

He shrugged. 'I hope you don't mind.'

'No, it's kind of you. And it really does help

take her mind off how bored she is.' She looked over at him, seeing that he'd retrieved the cutlery and the place-mats. 'Just stick the books on one of the spare chairs, or on top of the fridge.'

He glanced at the textbooks as he moved them, noting that the subject was paediatric emergencies. 'Is this what you're doing your special-reg training in?'

'Yes. It's why I spend Wednesdays in the children's assessment unit with Rhys Morgan. He's offered me a temporary post in the paediatric department.'

'Oh, has he?' Again, Max felt that twist of jealousy in his stomach and was cross with himself for being ridiculous. Maybe the consultant recognised Marina's abilities as a doctor. Just because Max himself found her incredibly attractive, it didn't necessarily mean that every other man would. For all he knew, Rhys Morgan could be gay and completely uninterested in Marina as a woman.

And he was even crosser with himself when Marina said, 'It'd be as maternity cover for Katrina, his wife—she's expecting their first baby in just over a month. They're a great team, and I've learned a lot from them both over the last few months.'

How wrong could he get? Not only was the other man completely straight, he was married. Preparing to become a father.

As Max himself had been four years ago. The news of Marina's pregnancy had been unexpected, shocking—and yet when he'd got used to the idea he'd loved it. It wasn't until the miscarriage that he'd realised how much he'd been looking forward to becoming a father, to having a family with Marina. To coming home and being kissed hello by a little girl who was the image of his wife, and who had the same love in her eyes when she looked at him. To coming home and teaching his son how to ride a bike and how to bowl a cricket ball. To telling bedtime stories and going to school nativity plays and sports days.

He pushed the thoughts away. 'Are you tempted to take the job?'

'A bit,' she admitted. 'But I know I'd miss the buzz of the emergency department.' She gave him a rueful smile. 'Maybe I'm just an adrenaline junkie.'

He smiled back. 'No, you're just used to being too busy. You were very good with young Jessie today.'

'Thank you.'

'And I was thinking, if you want anyone to do spot questions with you for the exams, give me a yell.' As soon as the words were out of his mouth, though, he regretted them. He could remember studying-sessions with Marina from her days as a junior doctor. And how he would reward her with kisses for giving him the right answers—but only at the end of the session, so he didn't distract her from learning... 'Am I keeping you from your books tonight?'

'No, it's fine—I've already done some studying. That's why I was running a bit late.' She grimaced. 'Sorry. It's a really interesting subject, and the time ran away with me.'

'No need for apologies.'

Supper turned out to be sweet potato wedges, chicken fillets stuffed with blue cheese and wrapped in parma ham, and steamed green vegetables, followed by bananas that had been studded with chocolate and baked in the oven, served with low-fat Greek yoghurt.

Max ate every scrap. 'That was wonderful.'

'It was just supper.' She flapped a dismissive hand and topped up their glasses.

Then he remembered something else that had been bothering him. 'What was Jessie's mum saying about seeing you in the paper?'

'I do a column in the local paper once a week. Milly in the press office talked to Ellen about it—' Ellen was the Director of Emergency Medicine and head of their department '—and she suggested I should do it as part of my training. The idea is to give people more of an idea of what we do in the emergency department and what they can do to help themselves.'

'Sounds good.'

'I'm trying to cover the most common cases and keep them as seasonal as I can—so I did Colles' fractures a couple of months back, and I'll do stings in the summer. It's a bit of a mix of first-aid advice and raising awareness of where else people can go for help—their friendly, local pharmacist for minor things, their GP or nurse practitioner for more serious things and us for accidents and emergencies.'

'Do you enjoy it?'

'It's fun,' she said. 'The only downside is that the paper insists on using my photograph. So when people do come in sometimes they're a bit wary of me because they're not a hundred per cent sure that I'm a real doctor.'

'Like that woman who was shouting at you the other week.'

'From what her friend said,' Marina said, 'she was deeply unhappy with her life and I was a convenient target for her to let off some steam.'

'She still shouldn't have taken it out on you.'

'It doesn't matter. You came to my rescue,' she said lightly.

Marina made more coffee, and shepherded him into the living room. As he'd suspected, the mantelpiece was crowded with photographs of her family, and the comfortable sofa was covered with cushions.

What he hadn't expected was the up-to-the-minute television and games console. He didn't remember her being into video games.

Clearly she followed his line of thought, because she laughed. 'I'm still not into "shoot 'em up" or car-racing games. But this is a lot of fun.' She gave him a sidelong look. 'Challenge you?'

'To what?'

'Up to you—there's a ten-pin bowling one, or there are some word games—or there's one that's full of mini-games, where you do all sorts of things, from hula-hooping to pretending to be an elephant. Which sounds completely ridiculous, but it's hilarious.'

'I'll follow your lead,' Max said.

It turned out to be enormous fun. Marina showed him how the controls worked; she beat him at the first couple of games, but as he grew more used to the controls he overtook her.

Finally, she flopped on the sofa. 'Enough! Do you want another coffee?'

'No, I'm fine, thanks.' He sat down beside her. 'I enjoyed that.'

'Me, too.'

He found himself staring at her mouth; when he glanced up, he noticed that she was looking at his mouth too. He leaned forward very slightly, intending to do no more than just touch his mouth to hers in a brief and sweet kiss. But somehow they ended up lying flat on the sofa, with Marina underneath him. Her legs were wrapped round his waist as he traced a line of kisses along her collarbone. How he loved her scent, the softness of her skin beneath his mouth. The tiny little noises of pleasure she made when he rediscovered a place she liked being kissed. The feel of her pulse beating strong and hard beneath his mouth, growing more rapid as she became more aroused.

Then he came to his senses.

He was practically making love to her on her sofa, when she'd invited him over simply for supper. This really wasn't supposed to be happening, and he was acting way out of line.

He pulled back slightly; he could see that her eyes were huge and dark, her mouth reddened from his kisses, and she was clearly as turned on as he was. Yet there was an undercurrent of worry beneath it all.

Was she scared that if she let him close again they'd end up making the same mistakes they'd made last time?

'Sorry. I didn't intend this to happen.'

She gave him a dry smile. 'Neither did I. This was really just an invitation to dinner.'

'And I've really overstepped the boundaries. Overstayed my welcome. I'd better go.'

But her legs were still wrapped round his waist and she hadn't moved. She reached up to stroke his face. 'Max, you don't have to go.'

'If I don't, I'll end up carrying you to bed and making love with you,' he warned. 'Because I still can't keep my hands off you.'

'Funny, that. I'm having the same problem. And, right now, you feel so good.' She slid her hands round his neck and drew his face down to hers, then touched her mouth to his.

As the kiss deepened, Max was completely lost. It was only when they rolled off the sofa together, she landed on top of him and all the breath hissed out of his lungs that he stopped kissing her.

'Uh. Remind me that I'm thirty, not eighteen,' he said.

She stroked his face. 'I'm not that far behind you. Only two years. Hey, do you realise that we're practically halfway to being pensioners?'

It was so crazy that he couldn't help laughing. 'I think we might have a way to go yet.'

She smiled at him, climbed off him and lithely got to her feet; then she held out a hand to help haul him up.

Except, once he was standing next to her, he couldn't stop himself pulling her back into his arms and kissing her.

'Enough of the teenage stuff,' she said with a grin when he broke the kiss. 'Let's finish this somewhere more comfortable.' She laced her fingers through his and led him through to her bedroom.

The room was painted soft duck-egg blue and cream; her double bed had a silver-painted wrought-iron frame, and there was a huge pile of pillows. Max could hardly wait to see her hair spread across them.

Except he still had the guilty feeling that he was taking this all too quickly. 'Are you sure about this, Marina?' he asked softly.

Her eyes were clear as she looked at him. 'I'm sure. Are you?'

He nodded. 'We're both crazy, you know that?'

She kissed him lightly. 'Stop thinking, Max. Let's just *be*.'

Telling him, in typical Marina style, that he was being too intense. That he should just relax and enjoy what was happening—because she intended to enjoy every second of it.

She untucked his shirt from his trousers and began to unbutton it.

Slowly they undressed each other, item by item. It took a long, long time, because they both had to kiss every centimetre of skin they uncovered. How much Max loved exploring her like this.

'I didn't tell you,' Max said 'You look lovely tonight—and I love your hair down like this.'

She smiled at him. 'Thank you. I can't wear it like this for work because it isn't hygienic.'

He couldn't resist playing with the ends of her hair, all soft, silky and curling round his fingers. 'It's still beautiful. Like you.'

'Flatterer.' But there were dimples in her cheeks, and he knew she'd appreciated the compliment.

She drew the pad of her thumb along his lower lip. 'You're still beautiful, too.'

He raised an eyebrow. 'Yesterday you said I was too thin.'

'You are. But you've also got the longest lashes of anyone I've ever met, and your mouth is irresistible. Sexy as hell.'

'So,' he said, stealing a kiss, 'is yours.'

Kissing turned to touching. And then they were in her bed, with her hair spread over the pillow, just the way he'd wanted it, and her head tipped back in offering, and he was kneeling between her thighs.

As he eased inside her, again he had that odd sensation that he was coming home. It was more than just familiarity: this was where he wanted to be. And they were definitely making love—because this wasn't just sex. It was a lot, lot more than that.

He still loved Marina from the depths of his soul. Always had, always would.

And he wanted her back in his life. For good.

Now wasn't the time to tell her—at least, not in words, but he could let his body do the talking. Rediscover where she liked being touched, what pleased her, what thrilled her. What made her make little breathy noises of surprised delight, what made her quiver and what made her grab onto him and practically hyperventilate.

As he felt her body tighten round his, the initial shimmer of her climax, he looked into her face and whispered, 'Open your eyes, Marina.'

She did. He saw the exact moment that she reached the peak—and it pushed him into his own climax.

*I love you, Marina Petrelli,* he said inside his head. *I love you.*

Afterwards, he lay on his back with Marina curled into him. 'So, what are we going to do?' he asked.

'About what?'

'The elephant in the corner.'

She pressed a kiss against his shoulder. 'If we're honest about it, Max, there is more than one.'

'Let's tackle the smallest first, then—this thing between us.'

She sighed. 'I don't know, Max. Maybe it's just a physical thing.'

It was more than that for him—and, from what

Rosie had said, Marina had kept other men pretty much at arm's length, rarely going on more than a second date. So it gave him hope that this was more than just sex for her, too. Marina Petrelli was warm, sweet and giving, but she didn't give her whole self lightly.

He smiled. 'I never could keep my hands off you.'

'Me, too.' She paused. 'I know this is going to sound mad, but maybe we should have a fling and get it out of our systems.'

That was the thing: he didn't think it would get her out of his system. 'We've already been there, done that and made a mess of it. And we made a complete mess of our marriage as well,' he reminded her.

'I'm not blaming you for that,' she said softly. 'There were faults on both sides.'

He hadn't talked to her, and she'd walked out. Neither of them had really given the other a chance to work it out. 'So what are we going to do about this?'

'Can't we keep it just between us for now?'

'Which makes me your dirty little secret.'

'Not *dirty*.' She shook her head in frustration, trying to work out the right way to say it. 'Just…I don't know where this is going, neither do you, and until we get things sorted out in our heads it's better not to raise anyone's expectations.'

'So you're saying this is just sex?'

'Yes. *No*.' She frowned. 'Max, please don't push me. There's a lot going on in my life right now, what with Rosie being in hospital and my studies. I really don't need the extra pressure.' She sighed. 'Look, what I'm trying to say is, I know we have issues and I know we need to talk about things. But I don't think tackling everything head-on is going to be the best way to deal with it.'

'So what do you suggest?'

'That we get to know each other again. Understand where each other's coming from. Learn to trust each other a bit before we tackle the tough stuff.'

'You mean, dating each other?'

'But *not* under a spotlight. Max, everyone in the department's lovely, but they're all incurable matchmakers.' As was her sister. 'If they have even a hint that there's anything between us, they'll have us married off faster…'

'Than we were last time?' he finished.

She nodded. 'Marry in haste, repent at leisure: there's a lot of truth in that. We didn't really get to know each other properly last time. We just leapt into—' She stopped as he burst out laughing, and frowned. 'What?'

'Did you hear what you just said, Marina? Considering where we are…'

Reluctantly, she laughed. 'All right, you have a point.'

He stroked her face. 'We managed to hold out for a week longer this time before we ended up in bed together. But we're not very good at keeping our hands off each other, Marina.'

'Maybe we should try a bit harder.'

'So there's going to be a rule about no kissing and no touching? I'm not sure how long that's going to last, but we can give it a try.' He paused. 'Are you off at the weekend?'

'Yes.'

'Got any plans?'

'Visiting Rosie and spending time with Phoebe.'

'Can you spare Saturday afternoon? If, say, I help you study in the evening?'

The offer was tempting. Incredibly tempting. She'd always loved studying with Max. 'What did you have in mind?'

'You suggested it,' he said. 'A date. You don't have to dress up, just wear something you can walk in.'

'We're going for a walk?'

'We're going to play tourist,' he said. 'Spend some time together. Get to know each other again.'

'But no touching and no kissing,' she reminded him.

'Not on Saturday,' he agreed. 'But right now I'm in your bed. And we're both naked. And what I really want to do is…' He leaned forward and kissed her, a slow, hot kiss that made his blood fizz. 'That's on account,' he said. 'Until we're ready to take it further.' He slid out of bed and retrieved his clothes. When she made a move to get up, he shook his head. 'Stay put. I can see myself out—and I think you need to get some sleep.'

She glanced at her bedroom clock. 'I didn't

realise it was this late! Um, Max, if you want to stay…'

He finished dressing and sat next to her on the bed. 'I'm tempted. Very tempted. But then I'll break this new no-touching rule within seconds. So I'm going home. I'll see you tomorrow.'

'I'm not working in the department tomorrow. I'm in the children's assessment unit,' she reminded him.

'Then I'll see you on Thursday.' He couldn't resist stealing one last kiss. 'Good night. Sweet dreams.'

Marina smiled as he closed her bedroom door. Yes, her dreams would be sweet tonight. Because they'd be dreams of him.

# CHAPTER NINE

MARINA was kept busy in the Children's Unit on the Wednesday, and after visiting Rosie she went home with her parents and helped out with Phoebe, but she still found enough time to miss Max. She didn't do anywhere near as much studying as she'd intended, either, because she kept thinking of him instead of keeping her mind on her textbooks.

On Thursday she and Max were rostered on different parts of the ward, and on Friday they were too busy to say more than a brief hello, but on Saturday morning he sent her a text.

*Your place at 1?*

*C u then*, she texted back.

It gave her half an hour to change her outfit three times and redo her make-up twice.

*Don't dress up*, he'd said. *Wear something you can walk in.*

In the end she opted for jeans, flat ankle-boots, a long-sleeved T-shirt and a light jacket in case it rained.

At precisely one o'clock, her doorbell rang, just as she'd expected; Max always had been the punctual sort. He, too, was wearing jeans, though his were black rather than faded blue, and his sweater was the same slate-blue as his eyes. He looked utterly edible, and she seriously considered grabbing him and breaking all the new rules.

'Ready?' he asked.

'Sure. Where are we going?'

'The weather's on our side.' He indicated the bright-blue spring sky. 'So I thought we'd get some fresh air, if that's OK with you?'

'Sure.' It was ridiculous to feel this shy with him. She'd been *married* to the man, for pity's sake. She'd ended up in bed with him this week—on two separate occasions, so she couldn't even say it was a one-off mistake.

But this felt exactly like a first date. A step into the unknown. Would they have anything in common any more, apart from that intense physical attraction? Over the years they'd both changed; would they actually like each other now?

She mentally shook herself, grabbed her handbag, locked the front door behind them and walked with Max to the Tube station.

'We're going to Kew Gardens?' she asked when they changed onto the District line. She'd never been to see the display of spring bulbs; it was one of the things she and Rosie had always planned to do, but they'd never quite got round to going.

'It's meant to be lovely at this time of year,' Max said.

It was breathtaking, with the fading drifts of daffodils and crocuses being replaced by tulips, blossom starting to come out on the cherry trees and the tiny flowers of the 'glory of the snow' turning the lawns near the Orangery into a carpet of blue even brighter than the spring sky.

She ended up hand in hand with Max as they walked through the grounds.

'I thought we had a no-touching rule?' she asked with a smile.

'This is our "first date", so I think holding hands is just about permissible,' he said, laughing back.

And, as long as they avoided the subject of the past, the old easiness between them came back. Just like on their real first date, where they'd talked and talked and talked. They wandered through the gardens and the galleries, stopped for tea in the Orangery, and Marina was shocked by just how quickly the time went.

'I know I said just an afternoon,' Max said. 'But can I persuade you to have dinner with me tonight? I'll spot-test you on paediatric complications, if you like.'

She laughed. 'I don't think it'll hurt if I play hooky from my studies occasionally.'

'So that's a yes for dinner?'

'I'd love to,' she said.

They ended up in a Chinese restaurant, sharing a mixture of dishes. And at the end, when they were thoroughly stuffed, they drank jasmine tea and broke open their fortune cookies.

'"Being happy is not always being perfect",' Max read.

That was true. They'd tried to be the perfect

couple, and everything had gone downhill after that.

'"He who climbs a ladder must begin at the first step",' she said, reading hers aloud.

'Well, that tells us,' he said with a smile.

He was teasing, she knew, but it was definite food for thought. If they were ever to salvage anything from the past, they'd have to start right back at the beginning—and learn that they didn't have to be perfect. That it was enough just to be themselves.

After Max had walked her home from the Tube station, Marina stood on tiptoe on her front doorstep and kissed him on the cheek. 'Thank you for today.'

He coughed. 'What about the no-kissing rule?'

She gave him a cheeky grin. 'As you said, it's our first date. I'm allowed to kiss your cheek right at the end.'

'Hmm,' he said.

'Seriously, Max, it's been a fabulous day. I really enjoyed myself.'

'Me, too.' He drew her hand up to his mouth and kissed the back of her fingers.

'What was that you were saying about the no-kissing rule?' she teased.

'You just said it was a first date and it's allowed,' he countered. Then his smile faded and his eyes grew serious. 'I hope that today's maybe a new beginning, Marina.'

'Me, too.'

'I know we've still got a way to go,' he said softly. 'And there are a lot of things we're going to have to talk about. But this is a start.'

'Like my fortune-cookie message said.'

'Exactly.' He stroked her face. 'Don't ask me in for coffee. We both know where that will lead. And, much as I want to kiss you right now, and carry you to your bed and make love with you for the rest of the night, I'm going to be sensible about this. I'm going home.'

She understood. Like her, he wanted to give them a proper chance. To go beyond their physical attraction and deal with the demons in their joint past. 'Thank you for today.'

'And thank *you*.' He waited until she'd unlocked her door, sketched a brief salute and was gone.

* * *

Sunday heralded a perfect spring morning, and Max called Marina to suggest a trip on the river down to Greenwich.

'I'd love to, but I'm meant to be helping Mum and Dad with Phoebe.'

'No worries. Some other time,' Max said. 'See you tomorrow.'

But the disappointment must have shown on her face when she ended the call, because her mother immediately asked what was wrong.

'Go,' Louise said when Marina explained. 'Phoebe has a nap in the afternoons anyway—and you have a full-time job in the busiest department in the hospital, not to mention the fact that you're studying for exams. You need a break. Call him back and say you've changed your mind.'

She did. 'Is that offer still open?' she asked.

'Sure.' Max sounded surprised—and pleased. Marina's heart gave a little leap at the realisation that he was looking forward to spending time with her. Just as she was looking forward to spending time with him.

'Meet you at Westminster at one?' she suggested.

'Great. I'll see you on the pier.'

When she arrived, Max was leaning against one of the lamp-posts, wearing black jeans, a grey sweater and a pair of dark glasses. He looked utterly gorgeous, and she wondered if he was aware of just how many appreciative female glances he was attracting.

Then he saw her and smiled, and her heart gave a kick—because that smile was only for her.

'Hi.' He walked over to her, kissed her briefly on the mouth and grinned at her shocked stare. 'Second date. We've moved from a peck on the cheek to a peck on the lips. That's the rules.'

'Oh, really?'

'Really.' He stole a second kiss, just to prove it.

He helped her on to the boat and held her hand when he sat down next to her.

It turned out the boat he'd booked was one of the fast boats, and they sped along the Thames. Max gave her a sidelong look. 'Feeling brave?'

'Why?'

'I have an idea.' He drew her to her feet and guided her over to the back of the boat. 'I know we're at the stern of the boat rather than the bow, but we have to do the *Titanic* thing, don't you think?'

'You're completely crazy.' But she loved his spontaneity; this was the Max she remembered from years ago. The man she'd fallen headlong in love with.

He stood behind her. 'Step up. I won't let you fall.'

She knew he wouldn't. And a few moments later she was standing there with her arms out-stretched, her hands entwined with his, leaning out into the wind. 'Max, I'm flying!' she said with a grin.

'Are you, now?' He drew her hands down, wrapped his arms round her waist and kissed the curve of her neck. 'Better not do the rest of the scene, as we're only on our second date—and we're in a public place,' he murmured into her ear. 'But I'm thinking it. Imagining it. Remembering what it's like to kiss you properly. Feeling your mouth open against mine. And then knowing that I'm going to carry you to our bed and make love with you until neither of us can see straight.'

Desire shivered through her and she brought one hand up to touch his face. '*Max.*'

'I know. Me, too. But waiting's going to make it all the sweeter.' He kissed the curve of her neck again, then stepped down, his hands still entwined with hers to keep her safe; they walked hand in hand back to their seat.

At Greenwich, they disembarked and walked through the streets to the Naval Museum, then through the park behind the huge, sprawling building and up the hill to the Royal Observatory. It was studded with the last of the daffodils, and families were out in force: parents strolling along with pushchairs and children running round. A perfect Sunday afternoon.

Max's hand tightened around hers. 'I thought that would be us by now.'

She stilled. 'Elephant alert.'

'*Enormous* elephant alert,' he corrected, his voice gentle. 'You're not over it, are you?'

The miscarriage. Losing their baby. Losing their marriage. The words felt too big to come out of her mouth. In the end, she said simply, 'No.'

'Me, neither.'

Marina was shocked into silence. She'd always thought that it hadn't affected him as badly as it had affected her. And, even though she knew that his mother's comments had been fuelled by jealousy and resentment, part of her had wondered if there was some truth in them: that deep down Max really was relieved that she'd lost the baby because they had both still been so young and right at the start of their careers. After all, he hadn't tried to get her back after she'd left. He hadn't followed her to London, hadn't called her… He'd just shut off.

'I know we didn't plan to have children quite so soon, but I always thought we'd have them,' Max said. 'More than one, because I didn't want ours to be an only child.'

'Like you were, you mean?'

He shrugged. 'I have no idea if my parents wanted more children. It's not exactly something I could ask my mother, but I sometimes wonder if they might not have been able to.'

That would certainly explain why Kay had clung so desperately to Max, Marina thought. If only she'd realised that she was gaining a daughter rather than losing a son.

Max had had all the pressure of his mother's love and expectations on him. And he'd missed out, too. 'Our house was always full of children,' Marina said. 'But when they'd gone I still had Rosie to play with. Sure, we squabbled—all kids do—but she was always there for me, to cheer with me in the good times and give me a hug in the bad times. She's always given me the space to work things out for myself and listened without judging.' She looked away. 'Rosie was the one who stopped me going under after I…after I lost our baby.'

He sucked in a breath. 'I'm glad you had her support. Though I know it should've been me. And I'm sorry. I just couldn't deal with it back then.'

Her throat felt too tight for her to speak. She made a noncommittal noise and rummaged in her handbag for her sunglasses, jamming them on to her face to hide her eyes.

He stopped dead and pulled her close, wrapping his arms round her, heedless of the people walking by them. 'Are you crying?' His voice was so soft that she could barely hear him.

She still couldn't speak, so she shook her head.

She wasn't crying…just. Though her eyes were stinging with unshed tears, and the pressure round her head was almost unbearable.

'I didn't mean to upset you, Marina. I just wanted you to know that I'm sorry. And I wish I'd been mature enough to support you myself instead of running away and hiding in work. I don't have any excuses. I let you down, and I'm sorry.'

'We were both young. What happened to us was a really big deal. Neither of us knew how to deal with it. And I should've supported you, too. I just didn't think it…' She couldn't finish the sentence.

'You didn't think it bothered me, because I wasn't the one who physically had to go through it?'

Hearing her thoughts spoken aloud was shocking. Particularly as she hadn't expected Max to read her so easily. There was an edge to his voice: anger, hurt, pain? She couldn't tell.

But if they were ever going to stand a chance she owed him honesty. 'Yes.'

He was silent for a long, long time. Then he whispered, 'The day you lost the baby was one of the worst days of my life.'

She could feel him shaking with the pain of the memories and the strain of actually letting the words out.

'I'd been worrying myself sick for weeks, thinking of all the things that could go wrong with your pregnancy, and part of me felt as if it were my fault, for reading up on everything and talking it up.'

She'd never even dreamed he'd felt like that. 'It wasn't your fault. Of course it wasn't. You know as well as I do that one in five pregnancies never comes to term. We were unlucky.' She choked back a sob. 'And it happened after we thought we were safe.' So unfairly. When they should've had the chance to relax and enjoy her pregnancy, to plan the nursery, talk about names and dream about the future.

'It wasn't your fault, either,' Max said softly. 'So I hope you're not blaming yourself.'

She shook her head. 'I'm not. I just wish it had been different. That we'd had our chance to be a family.'

'Me, too. I wanted a family with you, Marina. I know our baby wasn't planned, but I wanted a little girl who looked like you. And a little boy. I wanted to take our kids to the park with you, play on the swings, teach them to swim, read them stories. I wanted all of it.'

'So did I.' A single tear slid under her sunglasses and soaked into his sweater.

They'd wanted exactly the same things. And they'd wanted them with each other. So how the hell had they ended up like this?

'I should've told you,' Max said. 'I know now I should've told you how I felt. But you were in pieces, and I didn't think it was fair to lean on you and make you deal with my misery as well as your own. I couldn't make it right for you and I hated myself for being such a failure—at work I could fix things, but at home I was just useless.'

But if he had leaned on her she would've coped better—because she would've known that they were in the same place. *Together*.

'So working crazy hours was your way of coping?' she asked.

'Yes. And it was the wrong thing to do,' Max said. 'I know that now.'

'I had no idea you felt that way. I thought…I

thought that you were sick of me moping about, that you'd lost patience with me and I was being such a pain that you'd rather be at work than with me.'

'No. I'd lost patience with myself.'

She blew out a breath. 'I feel as if an elephant just sat on me.'

'Me, too.' He pressed a kiss against her hair. 'But we're still standing. And we're going to keep standing, Marina.'

It sounded as if he believed they could do this. Together. That they could lay the past to rest and start again.

Was he right? Or was this going to be her biggest mistake yet?

She wrapped her arms round him. 'No more elephants today, OK?' she asked shakily. 'I think that's as much as I can deal with right now.'

'Sure. We'll play tourist. Have some fun. The way it was supposed to be today.' He pulled back slightly, and brushed his mouth against hers. 'And I'm sorry I made you cry just now.'

He was wearing dark glasses, but Marina had a feeling that if he took them off his eyes would be a little too bright— with unshed tears of his own.

'We always knew it was going to hurt when we started dealing with the past,' she said.

'Like lancing an infected wound,' Max agreed. 'But, if we don't do it, we'll never get proper closure. Never really heal.'

'My mum used to soak sticking plasters off in the bath,' Marina said. 'I was never brave enough to let her pull them off quickly.' She raised an eyebrow. 'Did you tough it out?'

'Boys do,' Max said. 'And it's a point of honour not to say a word about how you feel. But I'm trying to un-learn that.' He raised her hand to his mouth and kissed it. 'Just not all at once, hmm? Let's live in the now.'

She walked up the hill with him to the Observatory, hand in hand; she stood on the Meridian Line and Max took a photograph of her on his mobile phone. She did the same for him, then he got her to stand in front of him, wrapped his arm round her waist, pulled her back against him and took a photo of them together, his cheek pressed next to hers, both of them smiling.

It felt as if they were courting again—just as it had years ago, before everything had started getting complicated. And Marina loved every second of it: wandering round Flamsteed's original observatory and marvelling at the Wren-designed interior; looking at the clocks, then wandering round the Planetarium and touching the four-and-a-half-billion-year-old meteorite in the entrance.

Max found them a little bistro for dinner, where they held hands under the table and fed each other morsels of their puddings. Then he saw her back home and kissed her briefly goodbye on the doorstep. 'Sweet dreams. See you tomorrow.'

'See you tomorrow,' she echoed.

'Tell me to go. Before I start breaking rules.'

'Supposing I'd like you to break them?'

He groaned. 'Don't do this to me, Marina. I don't want to rush into this. I want to give us a chance.' But he drew her back into his arms and kissed her until her head was spinning.

'Enough,' he said, pulling away. 'We have more elephants to tackle first.'

She laid her palm against his cheek. 'I know.'

He turned his face and pressed a kiss into her palm. 'Go indoors, Marina. Or I'm going to start behaving like Tarzan.'

She grinned. 'Me Jane.'

He laughed, then his face became serious. 'You're right about one thing, though: in the early films, Tarzan really, really loved his wife. And no other woman ever matched up to her.'

Was he saying…?

As if she'd asked aloud, he said softly, 'Me Tarzan.' He kissed her palm again and curled her fingers over the place he'd kissed. 'I'm going to fight for you, Marina. We're going to fight those demons together. And we're going to win.'

Life somehow had its sparkle back. All was more than fine in Marina's world—until Tuesday, when Max came looking for her in the cubicles, looking serious. 'Would you excuse us for a minute, please?' he asked her patient. 'Dr Petrelli, I need a word.'

She stepped outside with him. 'What's happened?'

'Rosie,' he said. 'Don't panic—she's OK—but

Theo Petrakis just called down. He spoke to me, as you were with a patient; he's not happy with Rosie's blood pressure and he wants to take her in to Theatre and deliver the baby.'

Marina's teeth started to chatter. 'Oh, no. Please tell me she hasn't had an eclamptic fit?'

'No, she hasn't,' he reassured her. 'As I said, don't panic—but she's a bit scared and she needs someone with her before she has the anaesthetic. Iris is calling Neil and your parents, but they're at least half an hour away, and Theo wants her in Theatre now.'

'Max, I need to go to her. But my patient!'

'Don't worry, I'll finish seeing your patient and give your apologies.' He took her hands and squeezed them briefly. 'I'll sort cover for you so you don't have to worry about a thing—just go to Rosie, give her my love and come and tell me how things are when you get the chance, OK?'

She nodded, unable to speak; she knew she should thank him, but fear seemed to have paralysed her vocal cords. She squeezed his hand, hoping he'd realise what she wasn't capable of saying, and headed straight for the maternity unit.

'She's OK, Marina, just scared,' Iris said, letting her onto the ward.

Rosie was shivering and tears were running unchecked down her cheeks when Marina reached her bedside. Marina wrapped her arms round her sister. '*Cara*, everything's going to be absolutely fine. I'm here and Neil's on his way, and so are Mum and Dad.'

'If I lose the baby…'

'You're *not* going to lose the baby. He's thirty-five weeks, and loads of babies are born at that age and are absolutely fine. And Theo's the best; he won't let anything happen to Bambino. They're getting you to deliver him a little bit early because you're not very well and Theo believes this is the best thing for both of you. He knows exactly what he's doing.' She stroked Rosie's hair. 'Take a deep breath for me. And another. That's great. And another. Attagirl. Keep breathing like this, nice and slowly.'

Finally Rosie calmed down enough to take her pre-med. Marina stayed with her sister until the moment when she was wheeled into Theatre for the anaesthetic, then she headed back to the maternity unit for a quick word with Iris, to find out the full situation.

A few minutes later, Neil walked in, looking distraught.

Marina met him with a hug. 'She's going to be fine. Stop worrying. It's just that her blood pressure went up overnight and they couldn't get it to settle. They've given her some steroids to mature the baby's lungs, so this is the best thing for both of them. She's having the section under a general anaesthetic, so we can't go in, but I was with her for the pre-med. Oh, and she gave me a message for you—she says she loves you.'

She'd hoped that it would reassure her brother-in-law, but instead he was shaking.

'Marina, she's the love of my life. I can't imagine being without her. If she doesn't make—' He choked off the last word.

'Of *course* she'll make it. We Petrellis are made of tough stuff, you know,' Marina told him lightly. But inwardly she was terrified; she'd read up on Rosie's condition and she knew all the potential complications—including the fact that Rosie could still go into an eclamptic fit even after the baby had been delivered. Not that she was going to tell Neil any of that; she could see that he was worried enough without knowing the worst-case scenario.

And she really, really wished Max was here.

'Let's go and wait outside Theatre. Then we'll get the news as quickly as possible.'

Waiting was awful. Although Marina started chatting, trying to take Neil's mind off the wait and the reason why they were there, he was monosyllabic and distracted. In the end, she resorted to going to the vending machine and getting them both a paper cup of coffee neither of them particularly wanted, just so they'd have something to do with their hands and something to concentrate on.

Time seemed to be moving through treacle. But then at last Theo emerged from Theatre. He was smiling broadly. 'I'm delighted to tell you that Rosie's doing fine and you both have a beautiful baby boy,' he told Neil.

A single tear leaked down Neil's face; he wiped it away with the back of his hand. 'I'm sorry. I'm being so wet.'

Theo clapped his shoulder. 'It's OK. I know how you feel—I cried like a baby myself when my little girl was born last year. It's the fear and the relief.' He smiled at Marina. 'I know women go through the physical pain of childbirth but, believe you me, men suffer right along with you. We worry all the time about what can go wrong. It's terrifying.'

'Tell me about it,' Neil said drily.

Had Max been this terrified when she was pregnant? Marina wondered. Being an emergency doctor, he'd know all about the potential complications. And he'd admitted on Sunday that he'd read up on things and worried. Had he worried about Marina developing a pregnancy-related condition, something life-threatening like Rosie's?

And then, when she'd miscarried… She knew now that Max had shut himself away in work because he hadn't been able to deal with the pain, the fear and the sheer helplessness.

She was aware that Theo was still talking. 'And if it makes you feel any better, Neil, my Helen was three weeks early and she's doing absolutely fine.'

'Can I see them?' Neil asked.

'You can see Rosie when she's completely round from the anaesthetic in a few minutes. We're taking your little boy to the special-care baby unit now, but that's simply because he's early, so he needs to be kept very warm and have a little bit of oxygen to help him breathe. It's really common with babies born this early, so try not to worry,' Theo reassured him. 'What I suggest is that one of you goes along with him, gets one of the nurses to take a Polaroid and then brings it back so Rosie can see him. It'll make her feel better, too.'

He smiled at Marina and rested a hand on her shoulder. 'And *you* can stop worrying as well. I'm not keeping anything back from you. I've given Rosie mag sulph, so I'm pretty sure she's not going to develop full-blown eclampsia. She'll be in for the next four days anyway, to give her a chance to recover from the section, and I'm keeping her under obs, but as soon as she's feeling up to it you can take her down to SCBU in a wheelchair.'

'Let's go to see Bambino,' Marina said. 'And

I'll text your mum and mine to let them know what's going on.' She swiftly texted both sets of parents to tell them that Rosie and the baby were both doing well, then took Neil down to SCBU. 'It looks much scarier than it really is,' she warned Neil as they rubbed their hands with the hand-sanitising gel outside the main doors. 'There will be machines and tubes and monitors and alarms going off everywhere, but it's nothing to panic about, OK?'

'I'm just glad you're here,' Neil said.

'Hey, it's what families are for.' She squeezed his hand.

Seeing the tiny baby in an incubator was clearly an ordeal for Neil; gently, she talked him through every single one of the machines and what they were for, to reassure him. Meeting the neonatal nurse who was looking after the baby clearly made him feel a bit better, but the clincher was being able to put his finger into the baby's tiny palm for the baby to grip hard.

'Do you see this, Marina?' he asked, awed.

'I do.' She was close to tears herself.

The nurse took a Polaroid photo of the baby for

them, and Marina took Neil back to the recovery room where he was able to see Rosie.

'Aren't you coming in?' he asked.

'No. You need some time together,' she said. 'Give Rosie my love—and I'm going up to the ward to meet our parents and fill them in. Take your time, and don't rush.'

Neil hugged her. 'You know, you're the kid sister I always wanted.'

'Stop it. You'll make me start to cry,' she told him. 'And, for the record, you're the big brother I'm so glad I've got. Now, go and see Rosie.'

Back on the maternity ward, both sets of parents had already arrived and were waiting in Rosie's room. Marina filled them in on what had happened, and made sure that all four of them had hot drinks while they were waiting for Rosie to come back to the ward, then headed back down to the emergency department to find Max.

'How are things?' Max asked.

'Rosie's in the recovery room but Theo says she's doing fine. She had a little boy.' She bit her lip. 'He's going to be in SCBU for a few days.'

'Which is pretty normal, given that he's thirty-five weeks,' Max reminded her.

'Mmm.'

'But you're still worried.' He stroked her hair. 'Honey, he's in the right place. Hold on to that thought, OK?'

She nodded. 'My parents are here, and so are Neil's, but everyone's on edge. Neil's mum has a cold, so she can't go to SCBU, and nobody re-membered a camera. I know it's a cheek of me to ask, but I said I'd get mine so the parents can at least have a photo of the baby. Would you be able to sort out cover for me for just a couple more hours?'

'Of course I can. But you've got some annual leave owing, haven't you?'

'A couple of weeks,' she said.

'Then why don't you take a couple of days of it now? I have a feeling Rosie and Neil are going to need a bit of extra support. You're not letting anyone in the department down—everyone will understand.'

'Max, I can't.' She looked at him, stricken. 'I want to be with Rosie and Neil and the baby—

of *course* I do—but it's my day in the children's assessment unit tomorrow.'

'Don't worry. I'll have a word with Rhys in a minute and let him know the situation so he can get cover. You said he and his wife are expecting a baby, so I'm sure he'll understand. These are exceptional circumstances.' He squeezed her hand. 'It'll be fine. Try not to worry. Give Rosie and Neil my love, and I'll call you later, OK?'

# CHAPTER TEN

EVERYTHING was a blur after that. Marina rushed home, found her camera and came straight back to hug Rosie and take photographs of the baby. Neil's parents clearly felt as if they could do nothing to help; Marina suggested that the grandmothers could go and get the photos printed and find some extra-small baby clothes, while the grandfathers went to the park with Phoebe, so Rosie and Neil could spend time with the baby.

'You're a genius,' Rosie said to Marina when their parents had left. 'Now nobody feels left out, and I don't feel that Neil and I have to stay up here and be sociable when I really just want to be with Nathan.'

'Nathan? That's a lovely name,' Marina said with a smile. 'And it suits him.'

She and Max had never got round to discussing names, thinking it unlucky until after the twenty-week scan. Except they hadn't made it that far. She'd lost the baby at thirteen weeks, the week after she'd been so sure it was safe to tell the world that they were expecting.

She pushed the thought away. Now really wasn't the time to brood. She couldn't change what had happened, so it was completely pointless dwelling on it; better to spend her energy supporting Rosie, Neil and the children.

'His middle name's Murray, by the way,' Neil added.

'Seeing as I was stuck in here,' Rosie said, 'it gave me plenty of time to look through all the baby-name books and find a boy's name meaning "from the sea". It's Gaelic.'

Marina suddenly twigged what her sister was telling her: her own name meant 'from the sea'. 'You named him after *me*?' Her eyes filled with tears.

Neil slipped his arm round her shoulders and hugged her. 'I don't know anyone else called Marina, so I guess we must have done.'

'That's…that's…' She was lost for words.

'Don't cry, *cara*,' Rosie said. 'Or you'll set me off and I'll start leaking everywhere.'

'I'll go and get us some drinks and meet you in SCBU,' Marina said, and fled into the corridor so she could give in to the overwhelming rush of tears. Her sister had given her precious baby the masculine version of Marina's name, showing just how much she loved her.

How she wished she'd been able to pay Rosie that same compliment three and a half years ago.

Later that evening, Max phoned Marina. 'How are things?' he asked.

'Fine.'

But he could hear the wobble in Marina's voice. Something definitely wasn't fine. Was the baby ill?

'Rhys sends his best and says not to worry— and he'll pop in and see the baby too.'

'Thank you.'

He heard an audible gulp, and it worried him even more.

'How was your day?' she asked.

'Fine. And don't worry about work. I've sorted cover for you.'

'Thank you.'

There was another wobble in her voice, and Max needed to know just what she wasn't telling him. The only way to satisfy himself about what was really going on was to see her face to face. But he also knew that if he suggested dropping by she'd say that there was no need and everything was fine. Marina always had been self-contained—too self-contained, really. If she'd cried her heart out on his shoulder instead of her sister's when they'd lost the baby, he would've felt that she needed him, that he'd actually been able to do something to help. But after that first horrible day she'd just withdrawn from him, and he hadn't known how to get her sparkle back. He hadn't really explained that to her properly at Greenwich: how helpless he'd felt, facing her pain and knowing he couldn't do a single thing to make things better.

'I'll talk to you later,' he said. 'Call me if you need anything.'

'Thanks. I will.'

Though he knew full well that she wouldn't. She'd try to fix things herself, the way she always did.

This time, things weren't so bleak, but he still needed to show her that she could rely on him. That he'd be there for her, support her the way she deserved. He went to the corner shop for supplies, then drove over to her street and leaned on her doorbell.

Her eyes widened as she opened the door. 'Max! I wasn't expecting to see you.'

'I think,' he said softly, 'you need a hug. Come here, honey.' He stepped into the hallway, closed the door behind him and held her tightly. She was trembling, teetering on the edge of leaning on him. And he really, really wanted her to lean on him.

'How are things *really*?' he asked, resting his cheek against her hair.

She shivered. 'Max, you know as well as I do, preemies can have real problems. I can't possibly tell Rosie any of this—she's scared enough as it is, without me dumping this on her.'

Marina was using up all her reserves to support

her sister; she needed someone to shore her up, too, whether she admitted it or not. 'Talk to me,' Max said. 'Tell me what you're worried about.'

'For a start, the baby's more susceptible to picking up an infection.'

'Which is exactly why they're so hot on hygiene in SCBU. He's in the right place,' Max reassured her.

'And preemies don't have the shiver reflex that full-term babies do. He doesn't have as much subcutaneous fat, he's at risk of hypothermia—and that can lead to other conditions.'

Such as low blood sugar, Max knew. 'Which is why he'll be wearing a hat, why he'll be in an incubator and why it's so horrendously warm in SCBU.'

'And he's at risk of developing RDS.'

Respiratory distress syndrome was one of the biggest risks to premature babies. 'OK, he doesn't have as much surfactant in his lungs as a full-term baby,' Max said. Surfactant stopped the small air sacs in the lungs from collapsing, so the lack of it caused problems for premature babies, making it harder for them to breathe properly. And the sheer effort they had to expend in breathing exhausted them, so they didn't have the energy to feed. 'He might need some extra oxygen to help him for a while, or if he's really struggling they might intubate him and treat him with surfactant—and yes, before you say it, they'll monitor the oxygen carefully. He's in the right place to get the help he needs.'

'And he's a high risk of developing apnea.' The condition made babies stop breathing for twenty seconds or more, and their heart rate slowed down below eighty beats per minute; it was most likely to occur when the baby was asleep.

'Not all preemies do. If he does, the nurses will stimulate him to breathe by touching his feet—and they'll put him on a monitor that will tell them if he stops breathing.'

'And he's more likely to have a haem—'

Max cut off the rest of the word by kissing her, nibbling at her lower lip until she opened her mouth and kissed him back. He walked her backwards into her living room, still kissing her, then sat down in a chair and pulled her onto his lap.

She stared at him. 'Why did you do that?'

'Because you're working yourself up into a real panic here, and that was the only way I could think of to stop you. Yes, there are risks, but your nephew's in the right place, and you know that— they'll be monitoring him really closely and they'll pick everything up.'

She dragged in a breath. 'He's so tiny, Max. He only weighs two and a quarter kilos.'

'That's pretty good, for his dates.'

'And his skin's thin and wrinkled, and his head looks too large.' She grimaced. 'I did a placement in SBCU, so I knew what to expect if he did arrive early—but it's so different when the baby's part of your own family, not just a patient.'

'Of course it is. You're emotionally involved— which is just how it should be.' He kept his arms round her. 'How's he feeding?'

'Through a naso-gastric tube. Rosie's expressing milk and cuddling him during feeds.'

'That's great. It'll help them bond. How's she doing?'

'Frantic with worry—it's not at all like last

time, when she had Phoebe naturally and could hold her straight after the birth. She's able to hold him for a little bit, but clearly it's not that comfortable for him right now, and she feels as if she's a bad mother because she can't give him what he needs.' Marina sighed. 'Obviously, she's staying in hospital for observation anyway because she had a section, and they probably won't discharge her until the weekend. I'm going to keep her company and support her with the baby during the day for the rest of the week, and Neil's going to try and delegate as much of his work as he can so he'll be able to spend more time with her and the baby in the evenings.'

'Is Phoebe going to keep going to the hospital nursery?'

'For the next couple of weeks, yes. She's going to stay with my parents, and I'm going to do the nursery run both ends of the day, to take the pressure off Neil, and also give Phoebe the chance to see a bit of her mum.'

'It sounds as if you've got it all sorted out between you,' Max said. Marina's family always had been good at organising things. Louise had been brilliant with the wedding plans, especially as everything had been such a rush, and Marina had been suffering too much with morning sickness to do as much as she wanted to.

They'd married in Kings Weston House, a beautiful Georgian mansion on the outskirts of Bristol that had been designed by Sir John Vanbrugh. His bride had walked down the amazing suspended staircase to meet him for their marriage. His parents hadn't quite forgiven him for not getting married in church—his mother had even mentioned Bristol Cathedral, at one point—but Marina had asked him for something simpler. And he'd wanted to give his bride the kind of day she'd dreamed about. The kind of day he wanted himself.

'Mum's been brilliant,' Marina said, and there was a hint of wistfulness in her eyes; was she, too, thinking of their wedding? he wondered. 'Neil's parents have been good too, but Neil's mum doesn't want to risk Phoebe or Neil picking up her cold, because then they won't be able to see the baby, either—and she's so upset, Max. She hasn't been able to see the baby yet, and photographs really aren't the same at all. She's trying to be brave for Neil and Rosie, but I can see it in her face. She feels useless and miserable because she can't do anything practical to help.'

'Maybe she can help with things like sending birth announcements and pictures of the baby to people,' Max suggested.

'That's a good idea. I'll talk to Neil and Rosie and see what they say.' She bit her lip. 'I just wish I could do more. I wish I could wave a magic wand so Nathan'll be well and ready to go home right now.'

'Of course you do.' He drew her closer. 'But you're already being a brilliant support.'

She swallowed hard. 'They're calling him after me.'

He didn't follow that at all. 'Didn't you just say they were calling him Nathan? Forgive me for bursting your bubble, honey, but Nathan doesn't sound anything like Marina.'

'Not his first name—his middle name. Murray. It's the Gaelic masculine equivalent of Marina.'

'That's lovely.' He stroked her hair. 'And I'm not surprised. Rosie thinks an awful lot of you.'

'I think a lot of her.'

He stole a kiss. 'Look, I live nearer to the hospital than you do. Why don't you come and stay with me for a while? It would save you a bit of time.'

She shook her head. 'That's really sweet of you to offer, but I'd rather stay here. If there's a problem, this is the first place anyone will ring.'

'You'd have your mobile phone on you.'

'Even so. I'd rather be here.'

With all her things round her—at *home*—rather than in his anonymous and impersonal flat. He could understand that. 'In that case, give me your spare key.'

She frowned. 'Why?'

'So I can help you with practical stuff. For a start, I can stop your fridge becoming like mine.' He kissed the tip of her nose. 'And I can work a washing machine nowadays. It'll take some of the pressure off you—and if you call me when you're on your way home, I'll have dinner ready when you get in.'

She shook her head. 'Max, you really don't have to cook for me.'

'I know I don't, but I want to help.' He drew her closer. 'I want to be here for you. You're supporting Rosie and Neil. Let me support you.'

It was such a tempting offer. Someone to lean on. Someone to talk to about her worries—someone who'd understand the things she couldn't say to her family.

But, the last time she'd needed his support, he hadn't been there. She'd had to put a brave face on it and go it alone. Until she'd fled back to her family.

Would Max let her down again? Or could she take the risk and trust him?

'By the way, I brought supplies.'

She hadn't even noticed the paper bag he'd brought with him. But, when he gave it to her and she opened it, she discovered chocolate. Lots of chocolate. And a box of tissues.

'That's so…' She was overwhelmed by his thoughtfulness. 'Thank you, Max.'

'Just in case,' he said. 'I had this feeling there was something you weren't telling me.'

'Not about Nathan. But you know how it is—

when you're a medic, you know too much. You know what the worst-case scenario is. I couldn't talk to Rosie or Mum about it without worrying them sick.'

'I'm glad you told me,' he said softly. 'And what you said isn't going anywhere. *I'm* not going anywhere, either.'

'Thank you.' Making the decision, she wriggled off his lap. When he looked wary, she took his hand and tugged him to his feet, then led him into the kitchen. She took her spare keys from the drawer where she kept them. 'You'll need the code for the alarm,' she said, scribbling it on a piece of paper and giving it to him along with her keys.

Max was as good as his word. Marina called him the next evening on her way home from the hospital, and by the time she got in he had a meal ready for her: baked salmon, new potatoes and salad.

'It's all pre-packaged stuff. All I did was follow the instructions and shove it in the oven,' he warned.

'It means I don't have to worry about cooking. Thank you, Max.'

'No problem. As I said, I just want to support you.'

If he'd supported me like that four years ago, Marina thought, if he'd let me support him, we'd still be together now.

The food was good, but Marina found herself picking at it. And she really wasn't in the mood for conversation; in her mind's eye, she could see her nephew in the special-care unit, vulnerable, fragile and struggling to breathe. As if Max guessed, he didn't push her to talk; he simply cleared away their plates and tidied her kitchen.

'Stay put. Visiting someone in hospital is tiring—not so much physically, but it drains you.' He handed her a mug of camomile tea. 'Caffeine's going to make you twitchy and disturb your rest. This might help.'

He'd sweetened it with a spoonful of honey to make it palatable, and Marina's eyelids prickled with tears. This was a whole new side to Max: caring, reliable, thoughtful. Just as he was with his patients and his staff. A grown-up version of the man she'd fallen in love with—a man who could still be spontaneous, but had a serious and responsible side.

The man she was still in love with, if she were honest with herself. She'd been angry with him, hurt and furious, but underneath it all she'd never really stopped loving him.

And she was beginning to think that he felt the same way.

On Thursday, Nathan's condition deteriorated, and when Marina met her sister on the unit Rosie was in tears.

'He didn't need those tubes yesterday.'

Marina knew that the nursing team would have explained everything to Rosie, but she guessed that her sister had been so shocked by the sight of the baby and the extra tubes that she was panicking. Gently, she talked her through the equipment. 'It's not hurting him; it's there to help the nurses look after him. He's probably a bit tired; this is helping him rest, so he gets stronger.'

'But it's all my fault.' Tears ran unchecked

down Rosie's face. 'If I'd rested properly, this wouldn't have happened and he would've been fine.'

Marina put her arms round her sister. 'This is your hormones kicking in, *cara*—it's the baby blues talking. You've had a rough time, what with being on bed rest and away from Neil and Phoebe for weeks, having an emergency section under a general anaesthetic, and now Nathan being in here. And *none* of this is your fault. It's just one of these things that nobody could predict—and Nathan's going to be fine. He might get a bit worse before he gets better, but all the nurses here are really experienced and they'll know exactly what to do.'

Marina spent the rest of the day with Rosie, re-assuring her, and was grateful to go home to Max's support.

'You know as well as I do that all conditions like this get worse before they get better, whether it's a premmie with RDS, a baby with bronchiolitis or a toddler with pneumonia,' Max said.

She nodded. 'That's what I told Rosie. But it's so hard to see him like that, Max. It makes me feel so helpless—I'm a doctor and I can't do a thing to make things better.'

'You're an emergency doctor, not a neonatal specialist,' he said. 'And you're the one who picked up Rosie's pre-eclampsia in the first place. If it wasn't for you, there might be a much darker scenario.'

She couldn't even bear to think about that.

'It's going to be fine.' He wrapped his arms round her. 'I'm here, and I'm not going away. But I do think you need something to take your mind off things.'

She tensed for a moment, wondering just what he had in mind.

But then he released her, walked over to her games console and slid a disk in. 'Prepare,' he said, 'to be thoroughly beaten and forced to admit that I'm better at ski-jumping than you are...'

He did manage to take her mind off her worries. He even made her smile. But as he prepared to go her smile faded.

'Try not to worry,' he said gently. 'I know it's hard, but Nathan's in the best place, and so is Rosie.'

'I know. I just can't…' She dragged in a breath. 'Max, can I ask you something?'

'Sure.'

'Would you…would you stay with me tonight? I'm not trying to make a move on you or anything. I just don't want to be on my own right now.'

She'd actually asked him for something—which meant she was letting him close. He'd give her the moon and stars if it were in his power, if she only knew it. Staying with her, holding her while she slept, was easy to promise and easy to do. Max wrapped his arms around her. 'Of course I'll stay.'

'I can't even offer you a T-shirt or anything.'

Because his frame—even though he was thinner than he'd been four years ago, as she'd pointed out—was so much larger than hers.

He rested his cheek against her hair and smiled. 'I think I can just about cope. Pink doesn't really suit me, anyway.'

To his relief, it made her laugh. Only a tiny laugh, but it was a start. Being with her was helping push her fears away—and it made him feel ten feet tall. Because he was making a difference. To the woman he loved.

'Come on, honey. Let's go and get some sleep. Do you have a spare toothbrush?'

'No, but you're welcome to borrow mine.'

She suggested that he should have the bathroom first. She was wearing a nightshirt when she climbed into bed beside him. She could've been skin to skin with him, Max thought, and he would have resisted temptation. Because he knew that right now she needed cuddles rather than sex. And he was going to give her exactly what she asked for. Exactly what she needed.

'Roll over,' he said softly, and curled his body spoon-style round hers. He drew her back against him, holding her close. She'd trusted him enough to show him her vulnerable side, and it aroused every single protective fibre in his being. 'Sleep, now,' he said. 'I'm here. And everything's going to be just fine.'

# CHAPTER ELEVEN

THE next morning, Max woke with Marina in his arms. Although he knew he really ought to get up, he couldn't resist staying where he was a little longer. Waking up with her like this, on just an ordinary day... Even though the quality of the light filtering through the curtains told him that it was raining, it felt as if the day was full of sunshine simply because he was with her.

The woman he loved more than words could say.

Not that now was the right time to tell her.

Eventually, she stirred in his arms and her eyelids fluttered.

'Morning, sleepyhead,' he said softly.

She opened her eyes, instantly awake. She'd always been a morning person, he remembered. 'How long have you been awake?' she asked.

'Long enough.' He stroked her face. 'I have to go, honey. I need to drive home before the rush hour starts and get changed for work.'

'And I need to pick up Phoebe.' She brushed a kiss across his mouth. 'Thanks, Max. For staying with me, last night—I really appreciate it. And I'm sorry I was so needy.'

If he wasn't careful, she'd pull away from him again, turn all self-contained: and he wanted to avoid that. 'Hey. I was the one who drove over here, all panicky and convinced something was wrong.'

'You didn't panic at all.' She smiled wryly. 'Nothing fazes you, Max.'

Oh, yes, it did. Losing their baby and then losing Marina had thrown him completely. And he'd tried to outpace the pain by burying himself in work. The second he'd stopped running—when he'd been immobilised in a hospital bed—he'd discovered that his demons had grown to twice the size. And he still hadn't quite conquered them.

'You'd be surprised,' he said. 'But we both have to get going. I'll see you tonight, honey.' He kissed her lightly and climbed out of bed.

'Can I make you breakfast?'

He shook his head. 'No time.' But maybe tomorrow. *If* she asked him to stay tonight...

Max was grabbing a sandwich at his desk during his lunch break, catching up on paperwork, when his mobile phone rang. He glanced at the screen, half-intending to ignore it, until he saw Marina's name on the caller display.

'Marina? Is everything all right?' he asked.

'It's fine,' she reassured him.

It was only then that he realised that he'd been holding his breath, fearing the worst.

'Sorry, I didn't mean to scare you. Nathan's doing a bit better today, so I wondered if you'd like to come and see him this evening.'

'Are you sure Rosie won't mind?' Since Nathan had been in SCBU, Max had stayed out of the way and concentrated on supporting Marina, not wanting to push in, and feeling that he didn't have the right to be part of her family any more.

'Actually, Rosie suggested it.'

'I'd love to.'

Did this mean that she didn't want to see him

tonight, though? That she didn't want him to cook for her, the way he had been doing—that she'd ask him to return her keys?

He made an effort to concentrate on his patients rather than his fears, and after his shift he made his way down to SCBU. He identified himself over the intercom, and Marina came to the door to let him in.

'I haven't brought anything for the baby or Rosie,' he said, giving her a worried look. 'I know soft toys aren't suitable for here, and—'

She pressed the tip of her forefinger against his lips. 'Don't worry about it. A visit's enough.'

It had been a while since he'd last been in a special-care unit, and he'd forgotten quite how high the temperature was set. And how noisy the unit was, with monitors going off every few minutes.

He hugged Rosie. 'Congratulations. Sorry I haven't brought you anything.'

She smiled at him. 'Don't be daft! I didn't expect anything—I'm happy just to have you here. You spent so much time with me before he was born, I wanted to introduce you to my son.'

'He's beautiful.' Max stood awkwardly by the incubator, not sure what to do. Funny; in a life or death situation, he knew exactly what to do, knew what to look out for, knew how to direct others. But here he was completely out of his depth. 'I didn't realise how small he'd be.' He grimaced as soon as the words came out. 'Sorry. What a stupid thing to say.'

'He is small.' Rosie patted his shoulder. 'Though he's not the smallest baby in here. He's feeding well and he's put on a couple of ounces.'

'That's great.'

As if sensing that he didn't have a clue what to do next, Marina said softly, 'Try putting your finger against his palm.'

'Is that…?'

'It's *fine*,' Rosie reassured him. 'Try it.'

He did so. And he wasn't prepared for the emotion that welled up as the baby's tiny fist closed around his index finger: the longing. The way his heart seemed to turn inside out. The way all his protective instincts reared up and made him want to fight dragons to protect this little boy.

This was what it could've been like for Marina and him: the first precious moments of seeing their baby, touching the soft, soft skin, seeing those blue eyes open in wonder…

Of course, he'd seen babies before. He had treated them, sometimes in the most appalling conditions. But it wasn't the same as seeing a baby who was close to you. The baby who, if he'd still been married to Marina, would've been his nephew: a blood relative of the love of his life.

He really hadn't been prepared for this surge of emotion.

Just for a moment, Max was completely un-guarded. And Marina could see how over-whelmed he was; she was shocked that someone so tiny and helpless could reduce him to utter mush. She could see the emotion flickering across his face: wonder, awe—and was that wistfulness?

Would he have looked like that the first time he'd laid eyes on their baby?

'He's beautiful,' Max said again, his voice slightly cracked.

'I can't wait to take him home.' Rosie bit her lip. 'I'm allowed to go home tomorrow, but Nathan needs to be here for at least another couple of weeks.'

'At least you can spend time here with him, and you're not going to be stuck on bed rest,' Max reminded her.

'That's true. And I can't wait to be home with Neil and Phoebe—even though I want to be here, too.'

Almost as if on cue, Neil walked in, carrying Phoebe.

'We'll go and wait outside—give you some room,' Marina said. 'Phoebe, when you've had a cuddle with Mummy, would you like to come and have supper with me before you go back to Grandma and Granddad's?'

Phoebe looked at Max, then at Marina; she nodded shyly and buried her head in her father's chest.

Max hugged Rosie goodbye and shook Neil's hand.

'Come and get me when you're ready,' Marina said. 'I'll be in the café.'

As she left the unit with Max, she asked, 'Would you like to have supper with us tonight? I'm going to make Phoebe's favourite—spaghetti Bolognese and garlic bread.' When he didn't reply immediately, she said, 'Don't feel you have to—we've taken up too much of your time already this week.'

'No, I'd like to—as long as you think Phoebe won't mind being around a stranger.'

'She might be shy with you at first, but if you're any good at building towers out of bricks that she can knock down she'll be fine.'

'I take it you have bricks?'

'I have a *great* toy box. Bricks, those little tray-type jigsaws, dinosaurs and a train set.'

He blinked. 'Phoebe's a girl.'

'She likes dinosaurs and trains as well as princessy stuff,' Marina explained with a grin. 'Let me get you a coffee.'

They'd just finished their drinks when Neil brought Phoebe in to the café. 'I've got her pushchair so she can have a nap on the way back to yours,' he said.

'And I've got a seat in the back of my car, so I'll drop her off at Mum and Dad's,' Marina said.

'You,' Neil said, 'are just brilliant. Thanks so much. Without you, these last few weeks…'

'And Max,' Marina said. 'He's been brilliant, too.'

'I know. Thanks for helping.' He shook Max's hand, then hugged Marina. 'See you later.' He strapped Phoebe into the pushchair and kissed her goodbye. 'Daddy'll be home ready for bath time, poppet.'

Back at her house, Marina dug out the toy box. 'Phoebe, Max will make you a tower while I cook the spaghetti, OK?'

Phoebe looked slightly wary and clutched at Marina's knee.

'What's her favourite colour?' Max mouthed.

'Red,' she mouthed back.

He smiled. 'Shall we start with a red brick, Phoebe? Except, I need you to show me the right one.'

'Red bick,' Phoebe said. She rummaged for a red brick and handed it to him.

'Brilliant. What colour shall we have next?' Max asked.

'Lellow.' She found a yellow brick and produced it triumphantly, balancing it on top of the brick Max had laid.

'Shall we count them as we put them up?' Max asked. 'One, two…'

Marina smiled, half-wishing she could stay to watch them, but then Max might feel uncomfortable and stop. 'I'll give you a yell when everything's ready.'

Cooking pasta while Max was playing with her niece felt odd, almost as if she had the chance to see what might have been. How their life should have been: simple domestic comforts wrapped in deep, deep love. She could hear squeaks of delight from the living room, the sound of tumbling bricks, and then suddenly Max's baritone rendition of a nursery song, punctuated with claps and giggles from Phoebe.

They'd both missed out, she thought. Phoebe on an uncle, and Max… Max on an awful lot more.

Phoebe insisted on sitting next to Max at the table. It meant that he ended up being splashed with spaghetti sauce, but he didn't seem to mind at all. And at the end of the meal he was the one who washed Phoebe's face and hands.

He was a natural.

What an amazing father he would have made.

'Do you want to come with me to drop Phoebe off?' she asked after they'd eaten.

'Better not. Things to do,' he said.

In other words, she thought, he was avoiding her parents. And she could guess why, too: in case they held the divorce against him, which of course they didn't. The Petrellis were nothing like the Fentons.

'But I'm off duty tomorrow. We could take Phoebe out, if you like—maybe to the Aquarium?' he suggested. 'Then Neil and Rosie don't have to worry while they sort out the paperwork before Rosie leaves the hospital.'

'But she's only two—how can we take her on the Tube?'

'I'll carry her. That pushchair's lightweight and easy to put up and take down, isn't it?'

'Yes.'

'Then, you handle that and I'll carry Phoebe.' He smiled. 'It'll be fun.'

A whole day with Max, doing parent-type things. In some ways, it would hurt; in others, maybe it would help to heal. To heal him as well as her, she thought. 'I'll call Rosie from Mum's and check it's OK with her.'

'Great. Unless I hear otherwise, I'll meet you here at ten.'

At precisely ten the next morning, Marina answered her front door, with Phoebe settled on one hip. The little girl stretched out her arms and gave a beaming smile. 'Max!'

'Hello, princess,' he said easily, and took her from Marina. 'We're going to see the fish. Do you like fish?'

'P'etty fish,' Phoebe said, still beaming.

'I think that's a yes,' Marina said. 'I've got her bag and her pushchair.'

Dealing with the Tube was as easy as Max had suggested, and Phoebe loved the Aquarium. She was entranced by the seahorses, and was wide-eyed in the tunnel where she could see the sharks. Max carried her on his shoulders all the way round the exhibition, pointing things out to her and getting her to count the fish and name the colours.

Again, Marina thought what a fabulous father he would've made.

If only.

Eventually, Phoebe's eyelids started to close; Max gently strapped her back into the push-chair, and found them a space in a café on the South Bank.

'What should I get for Phoebe?' he asked. 'Juice and a sandwich?'

'No need. I've got a packed lunch in my bag for her,' Marina said.

'But it's a warm day. Won't it all be a bit icky?'

'Ice packs,' Marina explained with a grin.

He grinned back. 'Duh. I forget how efficient you Petrelli women are. OK. Cappuccino and a panini?'

He'd remembered her favourite snack. 'Yes, please.'

He made sure that Phoebe's pushchair was parked safely in the shade, then went to fetch coffee and toasted sandwiches for himself and Marina. He greeted her with a kiss when he returned with a tray, and touched Phoebe's cheek gently with the back of his fingers. 'Bless her. I think the sharks really tired her out.'

'She usually has a short nap about now. I'd say we've got about another half-hour before she wakes up,' Marina said.

'Half an hour for just you and me.' He smiled, easing himself onto the bench next to her. 'She looks so cute when she's asleep, doesn't she? Mind you, I know someone else who looks cute.' He moved closer and whispered in her ear, 'Especially when she's asleep.'

Marina couldn't help laughing. 'Max, that's so cheesy!'

'Hey. I didn't claim to be perfect. But I still think you're cute.' He kissed her again. 'And, because you're the sexiest woman I've ever met, you can have first pick of the paninis. Brie and bacon, or chicken.'

'As they've been cut in half, how about a piece of each?' she suggested.

He stole a kiss. 'That's one of the things I love about you—you're so practical.'

A woman carrying a tray and clearly looking for a spare table smiled at them. 'Your little girl's gorgeous,' she said, indicating the sleeping toddler. 'Such beautiful hair. She looks just like her mum.'

'Yes, she does,' Max said without missing a beat. 'Thank you.'

His gaze met Marina's, and she knew they were both thinking of what might have been.

'Easier not to explain,' he said when the woman had moved away.

True. And she and Max were acting like parents—as if Phoebe were their own child rather than her niece—so it was an easy mistake for a stranger to make.

'When I first saw you with Phoebe,' he said, as he if he were reading her thoughts, 'I thought she was your daughter, because she looks so much like you. I saw the way you greeted Neil. And I thought you were a family.'

'We *are* family.'

'That's not quite what I meant.' He paused. 'It hurt like hell to think of you with a child.'

A child that wasn't his. It would've been the same for her. She couldn't have faced seeing him with someone else, either. 'It hurt,' she said, 'the first time I held Phoebe.'

'Because you were thinking of our baby?'

She nodded. 'I wish I'd known whether we were going to have a girl or a boy.'

'You were thirteen weeks. It was too early to tell.'

'But it made it so much harder, Max. It meant I couldn't give our baby a name and grieve properly. All I have are dates.'

'Valentine's Day,' Max said. 'And the twenty-first of August.'

The day she'd lost the baby, and their due date.

She really hadn't expected him to remember that.

Her surprise must have shown on his face, because he said softly, 'I hate those days too. And the only way I get through them is to go to church and light a candle for our baby. When I was in the middle of a disaster zone, and there wasn't a church or a candle anywhere for miles, I looked up at the stars and I thought about our baby.'

'I had no idea.'

He shrugged. 'You never asked.'

'Because you weren't there to ask.' She closed her eyes. 'Oh, hell. This wasn't meant to be a fight. I'm not blaming you for our marriage breaking up, Max. It was just as much my fault as yours.' She dragged in a breath. 'Why didn't you follow me to London?'

'I didn't realise you wanted me to come after you. I thought you wanted some space—and preferably away from me.'

She shook her head. 'I wanted *you*, Max. I wanted to know that you cared.'

He looked shocked. 'Of *course* I cared, Marina. I married you, didn't I?'

'Because of the baby?'

'No. I admit, I probably wouldn't have asked you to marry me that soon had you not been pregnant, but I knew from the first moment I met you that you were the one I wanted to spend the rest of my life with.'

Tears stung her eyelids. 'It was the same for me. But I thought you'd changed your mind about me. That when I lost the baby you realised you'd made a mistake, and that's why you didn't come after me. Because you were secretly relieved.'

He shook his head vehemently. 'I wasn't relieved at all. It broke something inside me, something that still isn't fixed.'

So he'd really meant it when he'd told her at Greenwich that he wasn't over it either.

'That's why you divorced me—because you thought I didn't want you?' he asked.

'I thought you wanted your freedom.'

He took her hand. 'No. I wanted *you*. But you walked out on me, and I thought you'd stopped loving me because I'd let you down. You stopped talking to me, Marina.'

'Because you shut me out, Max, and I couldn't get through to you. I didn't know how.'

'You were devastated about losing the baby, and there wasn't anything I could say or do to make things better. I couldn't cope with that.' He sighed. 'And I hadn't grown up enough to realise that if I'd admitted that, and told you I was as lost as you were but I loved you, then maybe we could've helped each other through it.' The lines on his face seemed deeper, etched in pain.

'You volunteered for extra shifts at work. It felt as if you'd do anything rather than face me.'

'At work, I felt I was making a difference to somebody's life. Getting *something* right. At home, I felt helpless.' He grimaced. 'Useless. I hated that, Marina. I hated not being able to help you when you needed me, and it was a kind of vicious circle. The more you backed off, the more I backed off, and the worse it got.'

'If you'd told me that was how you felt, I would've stayed. We could've got through it together.'

He laced his fingers through hers. 'Just for the record, you were the love of my life.'

Past tense, she noticed. Did he still feel the same about her? Or was he, too, scared of being burned again—scared to believe that this time they could make it?

'And I wanted our baby as much as you did—it didn't matter that it was an unplanned pregnancy.' He blew out a breath. 'You're right. If we'd talked, really talked, we could've worked it out.'

'We can't change the past,' she said, looking away.

'No.' He didn't say anything more, but he tightened his fingers round hers. Almost as if he were trying to tell her that they could change the future.

Could they?

Max came with her to the hospital to meet Rosie and Neil and hand over Phoebe. Marina wasn't sure whether she was more relieved or disappointed when he turned down her offer of dinner.

'We could maybe go to the park tomorrow with Phoebe while Neil and Rosie are visiting Nathan,' he suggested. 'There's a playground in the park opposite the hospital. Meet you at the park at ten?'

'If it's not raining.'

'If it is raining, we'll think of something else,' Max said.

But it turned out to be another perfect spring day. Max got Phoebe to count the boats on the boating lake and tell him which one was her favourite, and then they hit the play area. He checked that she was strapped safely into the swing before pushing her high enough to make her shriek with delight, and then, when she'd had enough, he grinned at her. 'Want to go on the slide?'

It was enormous. Marina eyed it nervously. 'Max, are you sure it's safe?'

'Of course it's safe. Look.'

There were other men taking toddlers onto the slide, walking up the snake-like ramp with them and then sitting the toddlers on their lap and launching themselves off.

'It's safe,' Max repeated softly. 'I won't let anything happen to her. Come on, Princess.'

He already had a pet name for her.

And Phoebe clearly adored him. She toddled happily alongside him and Marina watched, her heart in her mouth, as Max launched them off the slide.

'Again, again!' Phoebe said, tugging at Max's hand. 'Pease.'

'You heard the lady,' Max said with a grin, and did as the little girl had asked.

This was another side of him Marina hadn't seen. And, once her fear of Phoebe being hurt receded, she found herself enjoying watching them.

This was just how Max could have been with their children. And it put a lump in her throat; how much they'd both missed.

But she didn't want him to see her brooding. She forced a smile to her face and met him at the bottom of the slide. 'You're just a kid at heart, aren't you?' she teased.

He laughed. 'Yes. This is where I miss having

brothers and sisters—I don't have a niece or nephew to borrow and do things like this. It's fun, isn't it, Princess?'

'Fun,' Phoebe said, with a smile a mile wide.

If Max had stayed with her, Marina thought, he would've known Phoebe from a babe in arms. They'd probably have a child of their own, too, a cousin for Phoebe to play with.

As if Max realised the direction her thoughts were taking, the next time he reached the bottom of the slide he lifted Phoebe to chest height. 'I think Aunty Marina needs a kiss to make her smile, don't you?'

Phoebe clapped her hands, leaned forward and kissed Marina. Then she looked at Max. 'Max kiss Rina.'

'Your wish, Princess, is my command,' Max said with a grin, then yanked Marina to him and kissed her.

After that, he kissed her every time they slid down the slide.

He kissed her at every curve of the path through the park.

And he slid one arm round her shoulders as

they walked along, with Marina steering the pushchair and him holding Phoebe's hand.

It was a declaration, of sorts. And Marina wasn't sure whether she was more thrilled or scared. *Please just don't let it go wrong this time.*

# CHAPTER TWELVE

ON MONDAY, Marina was back at work. The triage nurse came in with her first case. 'Brianna's twenty; she's got a headache, feels sick, tired and dizzy, and her tummy hurts. I'd say she had the flu, but she doesn't have a temperature, and she says it's been going on for a while but she feels worse today.'

'I'll come and see her,' Marina said. She introduced herself to the patient in cubicles. 'Sorry to ask you this— and I'm not judging, I'm trying to narrow down the causes of why you're feeling ill so I can help you—have you been drinking or taking anything?'

Brianna grimaced. 'I don't feel well enough to drink, and I'm not stupid enough to do drugs.'

'Could you have eaten anything that might have disagreed with you?'

'I wondered if it was food poisoning but I haven't eaten anything dodgy.'

'You're a student, aren't you?' At the girl's nod, she asked, 'Has anyone else in your house had the same symptoms?'

'My flatmate's away on a field trip, but she's been getting headaches too. I'm sorry, I'm wasting your time. I've been to the doctor at the university health-centre twice, and they say it's probably post-viral syndrome, and that I've been studying too hard or something because I've got finals this year. They say third-years always overdo it and they have loads in with the same symptoms at this time of year.'

Studying too hard might make someone feel tired and give them a headache, but stomach pains suggested something else. 'How long have you been feeling like this?'

'Since before Christmas. I felt so rough this morning, my mum nagged me to go and see someone else.'

'Did the doctor say the same thing to your flatmate?'

'Yes.' Brianna smiled weakly. 'I'm really sorry. I'm beginning to feel a bit better now; my headache isn't as bad as it was.'

'Do you find this normally—your headache's bad first thing in the morning, and then better when you've been outside for a bit?'

'Yes.'

Marina had a feeling she knew what the problem was. 'Do you have any pets?'

'No, and I'm allergic to animals anyway.'

'I want to check something with a colleague first, but I'd like to give you a breath test and a blood test.'

'For drugs?' The girl looked shocked. 'But I just told you, I don't do drugs.'

'Not for drugs,' Marina said gently, 'for carbon monoxide. What you've described are classic symptoms, but I need to test your breath now and measure it again in a couple of hours to see if the measurement changes, and if I'm right I'll need to give you oxygen therapy. Do you have gas heating in your flat?'

'Yes, but the landlord's got a safety certificate. Everything's legit.'

'Do you have carbon-monoxide testers installed?'

'No, but we've got smoke alarms.'

'I have a hunch on this, and if I'm right I'll be talking to the council so they send someone out to do a carbon-monoxide test on your flat.'

'So I don't have post-viral syndrome?'

'No, and I'm glad you listened to your mum instead of dismissing it as nagging. I'll be back in a minute, OK?' She emerged from the cubicle and went to find Max. 'Can I run something by you?'

'Sure.'

'I've got a patient presenting with flu-like symptoms but no temperature, and she's been to the health centre a couple of times and they say it's a mix of overwork and post-viral syndrome.'

'But you don't think so?'

'I researched an article last year on carbon-monoxide poisoning, and I think she's a classic case, especially as she feels better outside and her flatmate has the same kind of symptoms. What are the chances of them both having post-viral syndrome?'

'Carbon-monoxide poisoning isn't exactly

something you come across in a disaster zone,' Max said thoughtfully. 'But I do remember a couple of cases at Bristol. Can you see the natural colour of her lips?'

'Yes, and she looks normal. I know it's when they're critically ill that the lips go cherry-red.'

'Check out the carbon-monoxide levels in her breath and a pulse oxymeter,' Max said. 'But you also need to check how long she's been away from her flat, because carbon monoxide has a half-life of about four hours in clean air. And if she's having arrhythmias or neurological symptoms it's better to opt for hyperbaric treatment rather than an oxygen mask.'

The test showed Marina that Brianna had higher levels of carbon monoxide in her breath than she should have, even though she'd been out of the flat for two hours.

'Carbon monoxide can have other effects,' Marina said. 'So I want to check how your heart's beating. I'm going to wire you up to a monitor, but it won't hurt. Have you had any fits or blackouts, or felt a bit disoriented?'

'No.'

'That's good.' As she set up the ECG, she explained what she was doing and why. 'Your red blood cells contain something called haemoglobin—it's what gives your blood its red colour. As it goes through your lungs, it takes up oxygen to carry it round your body, and you breathe out carbon dioxide. But, if you're exposed to carbon monoxide, the carbon monoxide bonds to the haemoglobin and stops it taking up the oxygen, so your body doesn't get enough. That's why you're not feeling very well. It also tends to make your blood vessels a bit leaky, and that's giving you a headache. So how we fix it is by giving you oxygen— basically it'll turn the carbon monoxide into carbon dioxide and you'll breathe it out.'

She checked the ECG monitor. 'The good news is that your heart's beating absolutely normally, so I can give you oxygen right here through a mask. The important thing is that you don't go back to your room until it's been checked over properly and the source of poisoning's been removed. Is there anywhere you can stay tonight, a friend's place where they haven't been suffering the same kind of thing you've been?'

Brianna nodded.

'Good. And I'm going to call the environmental health people myself, to make sure they do a test on your flat. I'll also be sending the results of your test to the health centre, and I'm going to suggest to the head of the centre that the team gets some training on carbon-monoxide poisoning.'

Over the next few days, Nathan became stronger; he was gradually spending more time without supplementary oxygen, taking larger quantities of milk and putting on weight. Max came with Marina in the evenings to visit him, and made a huge fuss of Phoebe. And, ever since Marina's hesitant suggestion, Max had started staying over, picking up a change of clothes from his flat before going over to hers, and keeping his razor and toothbrush in her bathroom.

It was almost like the early days of their relationship, when they'd first moved in together. And even though Marina was still worried about

Nathan she also felt strangely at peace. As if everything was finally starting to become all right in her world.

'You look happy,' Rosie commented on the Friday.

'It's been a good day—I had a visitor today.' She smiled. 'And we have a big box of chocolates in the staff room.'

'Who's been buying you chocolates?' Rosie asked.

'One of my patients.' She looked at Max. 'Remember the girl I thought had carbon-monoxide poisoning?'

He nodded.

'The environmental health people sent someone round with a carbon-monoxide tester and it turned black overnight. It turns out the gas cooker wasn't installed properly and there was carbon-monoxide pollution in the kitchen—and her bedroom, which was next door to the kitchen.'

'So, if it wasn't for you asking the right questions, she might have been seriously ill. Died, even,' Max said.

'Yes. It's good when things turn out right and there's a happy ending,' Marina said.

Rosie gave them both a thoughtful look. 'Indeed.'

The following Wednesday, Max was sitting with Phoebe on his lap, reading her a story while Rosie fed the baby and chatted to Marina, when Louise arrived.

Max stilled. 'Sorry. I'm intruding. I'll be out of your way.'

'You're not intruding at all. Finish Phoebe's story,' Louise said with a smile. 'It'll be more than my life's worth to take her home with an unfinished book.'

He finished the story, but Marina could see the wariness on his face.

At the end, he transferred the little girl to Marina's lap. 'I'll see you later,' he said.

'Max.' Louise put her arms round him and hugged him. 'It's good to see you.'

He looked utterly taken aback; had he really thought that her mother would push him away?

'Thank you for all the support you've been giving my girls. Rosie told me. And Phoebe's been telling us about the fish and the slide.'

'She's a sweetheart,' Max said.

'And she adores you all the way back.' Louise paused. 'Please don't feel I'm pushing you out, Max. Stay as long as you like.'

'I ought to be going, anyway. Paperwork,' Max said.

Louise raised an eyebrow. 'You sound just like Marina.'

'Funny you should say that. Actually, I need to leave, too, as I have some studying to do,' Marina said.

'Oh, *you*!' Louise rolled her eyes. 'Don't be a stranger, Max,' she said gently, laying a hand on his arm. 'See you soon.'

When Marina had settled Phoebe with Louise and said her goodbyes, Max walked out of the unit with her.

'Are you really studying tonight?' he asked.

'Yes, but that doesn't mean you have to go back to yours. I can work in the kitchen, if you want to watch a film or listen to some music in the living room. And I'll make supper for us.'

'Thanks. That'd be good.'

He didn't say much until they were back at her flat. And then he sighed. 'Your mother knows about us, doesn't she?'

'Guessed,' Marina corrected.

'I didn't expect her to greet me like that. I didn't think she'd forgive me for what went wrong between us.'

'It takes two to break a marriage,' Marina said drily.

'And it takes two to make one.' His eyes were intense. 'Marina, we're good together. These last couple of weeks…'

They'd been full of worry. But they'd also been full of joy, and a burgeoning understanding between them. After that first chaste night, when she'd simply slept in his arms for comfort, they'd given in to the overwhelming attraction between them. Right now they were so in tune, both at work and at home.

'Let's give it another go.'

The words that part of her wanted so very much to hear: Max wanted them to try again. To get back together properly.

Yet fear held her back, like icy water slowly seeping through her, and she didn't know how to stop it. How to make the chill go away.

'Marina?'

She couldn't bluff this. Couldn't fudge the issue. If they were ever to have a chance, she had to be honest with him and admit her doubts. 'I'm not sure,' she hedged.

He frowned. 'Why not?'

'It didn't work last time. If it goes wrong this time, I'm not sure I'd be able to pick up the pieces.'

'Back then, we were both completely unprepared to deal with what life threw at us. It's different now. We've both grown up. Changed.' He paused. 'Marina, I want you back in my life. Permanently. And I want to make a family with you. The time we've spent with Phoebe has shown me how it could be for us.'

'So you're saying you want children?'

He nodded. 'With you.'

'What if—' she dragged in a breath, remembering how desolate she'd felt when she'd lost their baby, how empty and lonely '—what if we can't?'

He took her hand. 'Marina, lots of women have

a miscarriage, sometimes even more than one, and then go on to have a baby. Just because we lost one baby, it doesn't automatically mean we'll lose another.'

She knew that—intellectually. But emotionally was another matter. Inside she was panicking, her stomach churning, still wondering: *what if?*

'And, if it does turn out we can't have children of our own, there are other ways to make a family. IVF, fostering, adoption—there are lots of options. It isn't just biology that makes a child ours.' His fingers tightened round hers. 'Let's cross that bridge when we come to it. But be very clear on this: if we *are* unlucky, if we do end up losing another baby, I won't shut you out. I won't use work as an excuse not to talk to you.'

Wouldn't he? She really wasn't so sure. 'You're going to have to put the hours in if you want to make consultant.'

He shrugged. 'I know. And senior consultant after that, and maybe even director of emergency medicine—but you and our children will come first. *Always.*'

She wanted to believe him. So badly.

But how could he be so sure it would work out? How could he be sure that panic wouldn't set in, making him react the same way he had last time?

Her doubts must have shown on her face, because he sighed. 'Life doesn't come with guarantees, Marina. Tomorrow, you or I could be knocked over crossing the road. So I can't promise you eternal happiness, and I'm not going to patronise you by saying that we're going to have a perfect life. All I can promise is that I'll try my hardest to make you happy—and I'll be right by your side in the good times as well as the bad.'

*Yes.*

She willed the word to come out of her mouth. And yet she couldn't utter a single sound.

'I guess this is a case where silence *doesn't* mean consent.' He looked grim. 'So that answers my question.' He took her spare keys from his pocket. 'I think I'd better give these back to you. And, in the circumstances, supper's not a good idea.'

She stared at him in shock. He was walking out on her?

'Goodbye, Marina,' he said. 'I don't think there's anything left to say.'

The fact that he closed the front door quietly, rather than slamming it, made things worse. He wasn't stomping out in anger: he was saying goodbye with a cool head.

It was over.

Marina had no idea how she got through the next week. The roster fairy at least was on her side, as she wasn't working in the same area as Max; when he was in Resus, she was in cubicles, and when he was in cubicles, she was in the children's section. The one time when she did need help from him—with a lumbar puncture on a toddler with suspected meningitis—he was perfectly professional, but he was utterly cold to her. No eye contact, no smile, and not a single word more to her than was absolutely necessary. And it broke her heart.

The only good thing to happen was that Nathan was discharged, and Rosie was ecstatic to have him home. Although Marina was genuinely happy for her sister, she wasn't completely successful in hiding her own misery, and Rosie picked up on it the second that both Phoebe and Nathan were asleep.

'You look awful. Is something wrong between you and Max?'

'There is no me and Max. We're just colleagues.'

The deadness in her voice must have been obvious, because Rosie simply put her arms round her. 'I'm so sorry. I thought you two were working out your differences. Phoebe said you kissed when you took her out.'

'We did,' Marina admitted.

'Then what's the problem?'

'He wanted us to get back together properly.'

'But that's good, isn't it?'

When Marina didn't reply, Rosie sighed. 'Why not?'

'Because.' Marina wrinkled her nose and flapped a dismissive hand. 'It doesn't matter, Rosie, you've got enough on your plate.'

'Listen, *cara*, you were there for me when I needed you, and I'm here for you now. And I'm going to worry an awful lot more if you don't tell me,' Rosie warned.

Marina swallowed hard. 'It didn't work out last time. How can we be sure it'll work out this time?'

'Well, there aren't any guarantees.'

'That's what he said.'

'Look at the last few weeks,' Rosie said gently. 'It's been a pretty tough time for our family, and he's been there to support you. He's even cooked you a meal every night, even though he hates being in the kitchen. Why would he do that, if he didn't love you? Cut him a bit of slack.'

'It sounds,' Marina said miserably, 'as if you're on his side.'

'I'm not taking anybody's side. I just want to see my little sister as happy as I am,' Rosie said. 'You never got over Max, and he never got over you. I know it was a mess last time—but you've talked through what went wrong, haven't you?'

Marina nodded.

'You've both changed over the last four years. If you'd lost the baby now, it would've been completely different—you both would've coped a lot better.' Rosie's eyes widened. 'You're not pregnant again, are you? Is that what you're not telling me?'

'No. Of course not.'

'So it's not hormones making you look like that.' She sighed. 'It's because you're missing him. And I bet he's just as miserable as you are. Marina, when are you going to stop punishing yourself—and him?'

'I'm not punishing myself. Or him.'

'No?' Rosie raised an eyebrow. 'What are you holding back?'

Marina sighed. 'I'm just scared that it'll all go wrong again, and I don't know how to get past the fear.'

'Then talk to Max, *cara*. Tell him how you feel. Because the only way you're going to work this out is together.' Rosie patted her shoulder. 'Remember that Tennyson poem I studied for my finals? He had a point: "Tis better to have loved and lost Than never to have loved at all",' she quoted. 'Do you really want to give up on everything you could have with Max just because you're scared of losing it?' She spread her hands. 'From where I'm standing, you're losing it right now. Talk to him, Marina—before it's too late.'

\* \* \*

Marina slept badly that night, brooding over what her sister had said. And at stupid o'clock she finally came to a decision: the only way to get past the fear was to face it head on. To talk to Max. Work it out with him.

Though she knew she'd hurt him. Badly. She owed him an apology before she could ask him to help her sort things out in her head.

But she didn't have the chance to talk to him at work, to ask him to meet her for lunch or after their shift. He was already in Resus when she arrived, and she was with a patient just before lunch when Ellen, the head of the department, put the department on alert for a major incident.

'There's a huge fire at a hotel just down the road—a boiler exploded and the whole place went up. So we're expecting an influx of patients with burns, scalds, smoke inhalation and possibly crush injuries; right now, we don't know what to expect,' Ellen said. 'I've sent Max out to head up the rapid-response team.'

It made sense, given Max's experience in disaster zones, but it also meant that he was walking straight into danger. Ice trickled down

Marina's spine. Fires were notoriously unpredictable. All it would take was a change in the direction of the wind, and he could end up surrounded by the inferno. And he might not make it back.

*Please let him come back safely.* Let her have another chance to apologise and explain, and tell him how she really felt about him.

She listened to Ellen's instructions about the procedures; she'd be working with the Resus team on the priority one patients, Eve was heading Triage at the main ambulance entrance, and they'd use the pre-prepared major-incident folders for all patients because there wouldn't be time to use the computerised system.

They'd just about cleared the reception area of patients when the first casualties came in. She assessed each patient as quickly and as carefully as she could, taking blood samples and giving fluids. Patients with burns needed plenty of fluids to support their circulation and avoid the risk of ending up with pulmonary oedema; during the first four hours, the extra fluid needed was calculated by the percentage of burns multiplied by their weight in kilograms, divided by two, so she double-checked the calculations to make sure.

Patients came in, already on oxygen and with IV lines in, their burns covered with sterile sheets. One particular patient had severe burns to his chest, which restricted his chest movement and in turn his ability to breathe. Marina had seen an escharotomy done before but had never done one herself; however, with the rest of the senior doctors busy with cardiac arrests and patients with severe inhalation injuries, she had no option. Her patient couldn't afford to wait. Although the experience was one of the grimmest she'd ever had in her years in the emergency department, Marina reassured her patient, cut the burnt areas of his skin down to the viable tissue along the line of his ribcage, across his sternum, and then made eight parallel-downward cuts. Just as she'd finished and her patient was able to breathe again, Ellen came across. 'Good job, Marina,' she said approvingly.

They were so busy that Marina completely lost track of time. She forced herself not to think of

Max and worry about whether he was safe—with his experience in disaster zones, she just knew that he'd ignore any risks. Wasn't that how he'd ended up with a house collapsing on him in an earthquake zone? Something that still gave him nightmares.

Eventually, the flood of patients steadied to a trickle, but Max still wasn't back.

She was walking through the reception area on the way back from the loo when she heard the news reporter saying that one of the rescue team was hurt.

No names, no details: but her first thought was Max.

And if he was hurt badly there was a possibility that she would lose him before she could tell him how she felt about him. Before she could tell him that she loved him. Before she could tell him that she was scared stupid about things going wrong again, but she was willing to take that risk—if he was still willing to give her the chance.

She headed for the triage area to talk to Roland, the ambulance controller.

'Roly, I just heard the news. One of the rescue team's been hurt. Do you know who it is?' Not caring any more whether the hospital grapevine would start to talk about her, she asked urgently, 'Please tell me it isn't Max. Please. I need to talk to someone on site to be sure it's not him.'

Max—tired and dirty after a very long day—walked from the ambulance bay to the triage area. He recognised Marina instantly and he could hear the panic in her voice as she asked Roland about him—panic, desperation and fear.

So did that mean she cared after all?

'Marina,' he said.

She whipped round and burst into tears as she saw him.

'It's all right, mate—no need to ring in to the RRT,' he said to Roland. 'We're all back now.'

Marina was shaking. 'Max, I thought you were…'

He wrapped his arms round her and drew her over to a quiet corner. 'In need of a shower and a cold drink, and some sleep, but I'm OK. It was one of the firefighters who was hurt, but he's going to be fine. What about you? It must've been pretty bad here, too.'

'Not like being in the front line.' She was holding him just as tightly. 'Max, if you'd been hurt and I hadn't had a chance to tell you—'

'I know,' he cut in softly. 'Me, too. I was just glad you weren't out there. I'd have gone crazy with worry about you. At least I knew you were safe here. Rushed off your feet and under a huge amount of stress, but *safe*.'

They were both shaking now.

'I stink of smoke and sweat,' he said.

'I don't care.' She refused to let him go, holding him more tightly.

'I need a shower and a change of clothes.' He rested his cheek against her hair. 'Come home with me?'

The word she'd wanted to say a week ago— the word she should've said a week ago—finally she was able to say it.

'Yes,' she whispered.

# CHAPTER THIRTEEN

THEY went back to Max's flat, their arms wrapped tightly round each other all the way.

'Have you had a chance to eat today?' Max asked as they walked into his kitchen.

'I had a sandwich earlier.' She had no idea how long ago it had been. 'But I'm not hungry.'

'Too tired?'

She nodded.

'Me, too,' he admitted. 'Which is probably just as well, because my kitchen's in Dr Hubbard mode. But I do need a cold drink.' He filled two glasses of water and handed one to her. He downed his in two swallows and refilled it, this time drinking it more slowly. Then he sniffed his armpit again and grimaced. 'I *really* need that shower. Come and wash my back?'

It was a ridiculously tight squeeze in the

cubicle, but she didn't care, and she could see on his face that he didn't care either. Right then they needed to have each other in their sight, just to be sure each other was safe. Tenderly, she washed him clean, washed all the smoke, dirt and grit out of his hair, and he did the same for her.

Usually, when they were naked and in a shower, passion would flare between them: but tonight it went deeper than that, emotion so raw that only gentleness would do.

Finally, they dried each other. Max pulled on a pair of clean jeans and wrapped Marina in his bathrobe. She held him tightly, resting her cheek against his chest. 'I'm sorry, Max. Sorry for pushing you away and hurting you.'

'So why did you do it?'

'Because I was scared. Scared that it might all go wrong again.'

'Scared that I'd let you down, the way I did last time?'

She dragged in a breath. 'I know I was wrong.'

'Marina, honey, what do you think I've spent the last few weeks doing?' he asked.

'Being there for me. Helping to take the worry away.'

'With actions, not words. Doesn't that prove to you that it'll be different in the future—that I've changed? That we've *both* changed?'

'I know.' She closed her eyes. 'But I couldn't get past the fear. Not until today, when I thought you were hurt—when I thought I might have lost you and I wouldn't be able to tell you how I feel about you.'

'Now might be quite a good time to tell me,' he said softly.

So she was going to be the one to say it first. To take the risk.

Though when she looked at him his expression told her the same as the words stuck in her throat. And she could see that he needed to hear it as badly as she did.

Given that she'd been the one to push him away, she was the one who needed to make it better between them. To say it.

'I love you,' she said. 'I thought I hated you at one point. But underneath it all I always loved you. A bit of me hoped that when you got the divorce papers it'd be like chucking cold water over you: you'd wake up, realise what we had and come and get me back.' She swallowed hard. 'But you just ignored them. My solicitor had to send them three times.'

'I didn't get them until I came back to England. And even then I wasn't in a position to sign because I'd broken my right arm and couldn't hold a pen.'

'But you signed them eventually.'

He nodded. 'I thought that was what you wanted.'

'I told myself it was what I wanted.' She sighed. 'I tried to move on. But nobody ever quite matched up to you. I always ended things after the second date.'

'Same here. I dated, and there was always something missing. It was because she wasn't you.'

She stroked his face. 'Max, we've wasted so much time.'

'In one sense, yes. But it's given us both time to grow up and learn what's important.' He dipped his head and brushed a kiss across her mouth. 'Do you know now that I love you and that's not going to change?'

'Yes. And I love you.'

'But?'

He'd picked up on her last doubts. 'There is one thing.' She bit her lip. 'Your parents never liked me, Max. I know you're close to them, and I don't want to make you feel torn between us. It isn't fair to them or to you.'

'You're not marrying them, you're marrying me—at least, I hope you are,' he said. 'Besides, it might not be the issue you think it is. None of my girlfriends before you were ever good enough for me either, in my mother's eyes. But this time I think she'll accept that I'm an adult and I've found the woman I wanted to share the rest of my life with.'

'Will she?' The words came out before Marina could stop them.

His gaze held hers. 'She's changed. A lot of things have changed. Even if the accident hadn't happened when it did, I would still have had to come home.' He paused. 'Dad had a heart attack.'

'Is he all right now?'

'He died. About two hours before I could get to the hospital.'

Marina stared at him in shock. She'd had no idea that Andrew Fenton had even been ill, much less that he was dead. Max hadn't said a word.

Then again, maybe he'd been too busy supporting her and hadn't wanted to burden her with his grief.

He hadn't had the chance to say goodbye to his father. Hadn't had the chance to hold his hand while he lay dying and say 'I love you'.

'Max, I'm so sorry. I know you thought a lot of him.'

'Past tense,' he said drily. 'It wasn't just that he had a heart attack, Marina. I found out after the funeral that it happened while he was in bed with his mistress.'

'Oh, Max. That's…I don't know what to say.' Not only had he lost his father, then, he'd also lost his ideals and had his family blown apart. She tightened her arms round him. 'That must've been so hard for your mother. And for you.'

'It turned out,' Max said, 'that he'd been having affairs for years. All those business trips… Half the time, he had another woman accompanying him. My mother turned a blind eye because— Well, I suppose because she loved him, and she hoped that if she put up with it he wouldn't leave her.'

'And it's why she clung to you so much,' Marina said softly, enlightenment dawning. 'Why she couldn't bear the idea of losing you to another woman, the way she was losing her husband.' She kissed him lightly. 'Yet she did lose you, because you went abroad. It must have been hell for her, watching the disaster zones on the news and worrying herself sick because you were out there. It was bad enough for me today, and I only had one day of it. She had three years of worry.' She blew out a breath. 'Maybe we can find some common ground this time round— because we both love you. And love stretches, Max; it isn't like a cake that you have to cut into smaller and smaller pieces.'

'I think my mother's beginning to see that that now,' Max said. 'Because she's found someone else. It's still early days, but Rupert treats her better than my father ever did. I think she's be-ginning to realise that if you love someone it's safe to let them go, because they'll want to come back, whereas if you smother them they'll pull away and not want to be near you.' He frowned. 'Maybe it's why Dad had all those affairs—because she was so anxious to be the most important person in his life that it made him feel trapped, and it was his way of escaping.'

'And it was a vicious circle—the more he did it, the more scared she became, the more she tried to bind him to her, and the more he tried to escape. Poor Kay.' She stroked his hair back from his forehead. 'And poor you. I know you looked up to your dad.'

'He wasn't who I thought he was.' Max lifted a shoulder in a half-shrug. 'I had plenty of time to think about it.'

'While you were stuck in a hospital bed.'

'I wasn't the best of patients,' Max admitted.

'Medics never are—and you'd already had enough dumped on you. Being hurt so you couldn't work, your father dying and then having to deal with all the emotional fallout of what you'd learned.'

'I stopped believing in love and marriage for a while.' He stroked her face. 'Though your family's restored my faith there.'

'I'm glad.' She bit her lip. 'Though it couldn't have helped, having divorce papers waiting for you when you got back to England.'

'When I finally opened them, I was livid. I had a fit and threw them over the other side of the room,' Max said ruefully. 'Except then, because of my leg, I couldn't get down to pick them up again. Luckily a friend came in to visit me before my mother did, and she got rid of the evidence for me.'

*'She?'*

'It's possible for a man to have female friends,' Max said. 'And, believe me, I was in no fit state to think about anything more than friendship. I was either stuck in traction or stuck in a wheelchair.'

Max wasn't the still, quiet sort. He was happiest in the thick of action. 'It must have driven you crazy.'

'It did. I had hours and hours and hours with nothing to do except brood. I thought of you—a lot. And ranted a bit. Your ears must've been burning.'

'I ranted about you, too,' Marina admitted.

'I was so sure I hated you,' Max said. 'And then

I came to London and opened that curtain and saw you.'

'In all the emergency departments in all the world, you had to walk into mine,' she quipped.

'Yup. And then I discovered that, actually, I didn't hate you. That was just a mask, a way of coping with what I'd lost. I couldn't keep my eyes off you. And when I thought that Neil was your husband… Well, put it this way, my physio would've taken me to task for overdoing it at the gym that evening.'

'Oh, Max.'

'And you wore those jeans to taunt me at the bowling alley.'

'My jeans are perfectly respectable,' Marina said. 'Besides, I didn't know you were going to be there that night. Might I point out that *you* were wearing soft, very touchable denims yourself?'

A teasing glint lit his eyes. 'You wanted to touch me, then?'

'I wanted to take you home, rip your clothes off and have my wicked way with you,' Marina said.

The glint intensified. 'I seem to remember you did that a few days later. In my flat. Come to think of it, not very far from where we are right now.'

'This isn't home,' Marina said.

'Actually, it is.' He leaned forward and stole a kiss. 'Home's wherever *you* are. Everything else is just trappings.' He stroked her face. 'I think we've been given a second chance. Are you brave enough to take it?'

This time, she didn't hesitate. Didn't need to. 'Yes,' she said. 'Because I know you'll be there right beside me.'

His kiss was warm and sweet and full of promise.

'So, are we going to take it steady this time? Court each other all over again?' she asked.

'Not on your life,' Max said. 'I've spent four years missing you, and the last week in the uttermost reaches of hell. I want you back in my life permanently, starting right now.'

'Marry in haste…' she warned him. 'Didn't you learn that last time round?'

'We don't have to set a date right now. Actually, you don't even have to marry me, if you don't want to.' His eyes were very, very blue, full of sincerity and love. 'Just be with me,

Marina. You're the love of my life; I've missed you so much that it hurt even to breathe, and I don't want to spend any more time without you. I don't care where we live, or whether you call yourself Fenton or Petrelli. I just want you back with me. For good. And starting right now.' He paused. 'One more thing: we talk. Even if we think what we say might be upsetting, if we're unhappy about something, we talk about it. No hiding in work. Deal?'

'Deal.' And she sealed it with a kiss.

# EPILOGUE

*Fourteen months later*

'How did we get to be so lucky?' Max asked, coming to stand behind Marina and wrapping his arms round her waist. He rested his chin on her shoulder and looked through the kitchen window to the garden. His mother and Marina's were sitting next to each other in the shade, chatting away and cooing over Carly Rosamond Fenton, the youngest member of the family. Rupert, his mother's partner, was manning the barbecue with Marina's father. Rosie was taking dishes of salad through to the huge table set ready for lunch under the gazebo, and Neil and various Petrelli aunts, uncles and cousins were chatting in groups and playing with the children.

Max had grown up with a small, intense

family. Now he was part of a huge, noisy one that believed in fun and love and laughter—and his mother and Rupert had been accepted right along with him. Over the last year his mother had relaxed, discovering that she wasn't losing a son but gaining a daughter, and a whole new family to boot. Marina had made a point of sitting down and talking with her, and making her realise that she was always going to be part of their lives—that there would be room for her.

'I think,' Marina said, turning round in his arms and kissing him, 'That we make our own luck.'

'Tut tut. Put each other down, you two,' Rosie teased from the doorway to the garden. 'You're supposed to be getting drinks, Max. And you're supposed to be sorting out the buns for the burgers and the rolls for the hotdogs,' she told her sister. 'Dad and Rupert sent me in to find out where you'd got to because everything's almost ready.'

Marina laughed. 'Is it my fault that I have the sexiest husband in the world? He distracted me.'

'On the contrary, *you* distracted *me*,' Max countered. 'So I think that deserves a forfeit.' He stole another kiss.

Rosie spread her hands. 'Honestly, you two. Anyone would think that you were newlyweds!'

'We are. We only got married a year ago today,' Marina said.

'And what a year it's been,' Max said softly. Marrying the love of his life; being promoted to consultant in a unit where he was most definitely part of the team. And becoming a father to a baby girl who'd taught him that the Petrellis knew exactly what they were talking about: love stretched and grew along with the family. 'Life doesn't get any better than this.'

'Tell me that in twenty-five years,' Rosie said. 'When we're celebrating your silver wedding and you've got grandchildren in your arms.'

Max looked at his wife and smiled. 'You know, I think you might just be right...'

# MEDICAL™

## Large Print

*Titles for the next six months…*

### *October*

| | |
|---|---|
| THE NURSE'S BROODING BOSS | Laura Iding |
| EMERGENCY DOCTOR AND CINDERELLA | Melanie Milburne |
| CITY SURGEON, SMALL TOWN MIRACLE | Marion Lennox |
| BACHELOR DAD, GIRL NEXT DOOR | Sharon Archer |
| A BABY FOR THE FLYING DOCTOR | Lucy Clark |
| NURSE, NANNY…BRIDE! | Alison Roberts |

### *November*

| | |
|---|---|
| THE SURGEON'S MIRACLE | Caroline Anderson |
| DR DI ANGELO'S BABY BOMBSHELL | Janice Lynn |
| NEWBORN NEEDS A DAD | Dianne Drake |
| HIS MOTHERLESS LITTLE TWINS | Dianne Drake |
| WEDDING BELLS FOR THE VILLAGE NURSE | Abigail Gordon |
| HER LONG-LOST HUSBAND | Josie Metcalfe |

### *December*

| | |
|---|---|
| THE MIDWIFE AND THE MILLIONAIRE | Fiona McArthur |
| FROM SINGLE MUM TO LADY | Judy Campbell |
| KNIGHT ON THE CHILDREN'S WARD | Carol Marinelli |
| CHILDREN'S DOCTOR, SHY NURSE | Molly Evans |
| HAWAIIAN SUNSET, DREAM PROPOSAL | Joanna Neil |
| RESCUED: MOTHER AND BABY | Anne Fraser |

 MILLS & BOON®

# MEDICAL™

## Large Print

### *January*

| | |
|---|---|
| DARE SHE DATE THE DREAMY DOC? | Sarah Morgan |
| DR DROP-DEAD GORGEOUS | Emily Forbes |
| HER BROODING ITALIAN SURGEON | Fiona Lowe |
| A FATHER FOR BABY ROSE | Margaret Barker |
| NEUROSURGEON…AND MUM! | Kate Hardy |
| WEDDING IN DARLING DOWNS | Leah Martyn |

### *February*

| | |
|---|---|
| WISHING FOR A MIRACLE | Alison Roberts |
| THE MARRY-ME WISH | Alison Roberts |
| PRINCE CHARMING OF HARLEY STREET | Anne Fraser |
| THE HEART DOCTOR AND THE BABY | Lynne Marshall |
| THE SECRET DOCTOR | Joanna Neil |
| THE DOCTOR'S DOUBLE TROUBLE | Lucy Clark |

### *March*

| | |
|---|---|
| DATING THE MILLIONAIRE DOCTOR | Marion Lennox |
| ALESSANDRO AND THE CHEERY NANNY | Amy Andrews |
| VALENTINO'S PREGNANCY BOMBSHELL | Amy Andrews |
| A KNIGHT FOR NURSE HART | Laura Iding |
| A NURSE TO TAME THE PLAYBOY | Maggie Kingsley |
| VILLAGE MIDWIFE, BLUSHING BRIDE | Gill Sanderson |

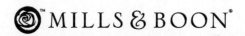

MILLS & BOON®